THE GOOD VIRUS

Govind S. Mattay

Order this book online at www.trafford.com
or email orders@trafford.com

Most Trafford titles are also available at major online book retailers.

© Copyright 2014 Govind S. Mattay.
All rights reserved. No part of this publication may be reproduced,
stored in a retrieval system, or transmitted, in any form or by
any means, electronic, mechanical, photocopying, recording, or
otherwise, without the written prior permission of the author.

Print information available on the last page.

ISBN: 978-1-4907-4683-8 (sc)
ISBN: 978-1-4907-4682-1 (e)

Library of Congress Control Number: 2014916811

Because of the dynamic nature of the Internet, any web addresses or
links contained in this book may have changed since publication and
may no longer be valid. The views expressed in this work are solely those
of the author and do not necessarily reflect the views of the publisher,
and the publisher hereby disclaims any responsibility for them.

Any people depicted in stock imagery provided by Thinkstock are models,
and such images are being used for illustrative purposes only.
Certain stock imagery © Thinkstock.

Trafford rev. 03/20/2015

 www.trafford.com

North America & international
toll-free: 1 888 232 4444 (USA & Canada)
fax: 812 355 4082

ACKNOWLEDGMENT

"I want to thank my family, Neeraja, Anand, and Raghav Mattay, for all of their help along the way."

-Govind S. Mattay

DEDICATION

"I would like to dedicate this book to my two little cousins, Mallika and Tejasvi Charagundla."

-Govind S. Mattay

PROLOGUE

Memories flashed through Samir's head. He was running, running very fast. Bleak metallic walls surrounded him in a tight corridor. Fluorescent lights shone brightly upon his face drenched with sweat. It seemed as if he was a lab rat bounding hopelessly through a meandering maze. There were no openings to be seen and the corridor looked exactly the same. Was he running in circles?

As soon as he rounded a corner, he noticed something different. The metal color became darker and the lights dimmed. The temperature shot down and it became extremely chilly. Maybe he was traveling deeper and deeper underground. He also spotted a video camera fixed upon him in the corner of the hallway. Now he knew for sure he was being watched. At least one thing was good: he wasn't running in circles.

He heard a noise. The sound of rubber soles padding against metal resounded through the corridor. Was someone after him? His pulse quickened and adrenaline rushed through his veins. He started to run at maximum speed as the air whipped at his face. Dizziness from exhaustion and dehydration swept over him. He was being chased!

Soon his breath was heavy. He took deep gasps of the frigid air, trying to take in as much oxygen as possible. How much more of this could he take?

Suddenly his surroundings changed. He was no longer in a claustrophobic hallway but in a large spacious room. The dark gray metal changed into lavender tiles. Large vats filled with some type of liquid were spread throughout the room. Test tubes of the same clear liquid were placed in holders. He wanted time to look around but his pursuers were hard on his heels!

Unexpectedly, a giant of a man tackled him, pinning him to the ground. He strained to get a good look at his pursuer, but could only capture a glimpse before being knocked down again. The man was Caucasian, brawny, strikingly hairless, and had piercing blue eyes. As he was being tackled, Samir noticed a deep scar running down the man's hand and forearm. Then a brown-haired man with a large forehead appeared and pulled a syringe from his white coat. "You have seen too much," the man stated. The last thing Samir saw was the name "Vaccine Corp" painted in large black letters upon the wall. A spark of recognition shot through his brain before the man injected him with the syringe and he fell into a dark dreamless slumber.

CHAPTER 1

Veer was miserable. He stared at the yellow and red tiled floor of Medley Middle School while walking to his locker on the second floor. Today was his first day of junior high. Many kids were excited about this, but not him. Middle school just meant more bullies to watch out for, more kids to embarrass himself in front of, and worst of all, a grueling gym class every single day.

First, he had to walk to the other side of the school to find the stairs. Veer paid close attention to where he was, for Medley was a huge school, and he didn't want to get lost on the first day of the school year. As he walked, he noticed all the colorful signs posted on the bulletin boards beside classrooms. Some read "Welcome 7TH and 8TH graders!" Others said "We are going to have a fantastic year!"

A huge influx of kids came storming down the once empty hallway like a herd of buffalo. The mere force of them knocked Veer off his feet and he fell to the cold floor. They didn't even bother to move around him, but just trampled right over him. "Bus number 52 has just arrived," the monotone voice of the school secretary boomed through the speakers.

"You could have told me earlier," Veer muttered to himself while getting up and brushing the dirt off his new and now stained collared shirt. His first day of school was already a disaster.

"Aww, a little sevy got a boo-boo!" a voice called from down the hall. Veer looked up to see three eighth-grade boys in ripped jeans and black leather jackets marching toward him. Just the thing to make his day worse: bullies.

"Do you know what today is, punk?" the tallest eighth grader asked him.

"Tuesday?" Veer responded.

"Wrong, idiot. It's Sevy-Bop Day!" With that, the eighth grader smashed him on the head with his fist and walked away laughing.

Veer was slow to recover, rubbing his head to soothe the pain. This day was just getting worse. His first days of school were always bad, but this was a new record: two catastrophes in a matter of minutes.

After slowly collecting his books off the floor, Veer set off once more to find his locker. Soon he reached the stairs and started to climb them one at a time.

As soon as he reached the double doorway, Veer turned left and headed down a hall lined with old rusty lockers. It was just Veer's luck for his locker to be in the only part of the school that wasn't refurbished in the recent renovation. As he approached his locker, the very last one in the huge hall, he dug deep into his pockets and pulled out a tiny piece of paper that contained his lock code. Veer strained to recognize the numbers that were scribbled upon the paper in his messy handwriting. He luckily managed to figure out two of the numbers, but wasn't sure if the third was a 2 or a 3. He'd just have to try both codes to get his locker open. *Now how did it go? Turn left to 33, then right all the way around and back to 17, then left again? No that wasn't right. It was the opposite. Right, left, right. Yeah, that was the way.* After trying the first code, the locker didn't open. Veer had better luck the second try as the lock clicked loose. But now there was a different problem, the locker was jammed stuck. It took another three attempts before the locker suddenly flew open and Veer fell to the floor. He pushed himself onto his feet and deposited his books in the ancient rusty locker. Now it was time for the beginning-of-school assembly.

After traveling through the hallway and down the stairs, Veer once again heard the nasal monotone voice of the school secretary from the speakers.

It squeaked, "All seventh and eighth graders report to the gymnasium for the beginning-of-school assembly. All seventh and eighth graders report to the gymnasium for the beginning-of-school assembly. Thank you."

Suddenly there was a murmur of voices and a soft thumping of feet. It was like in the movies when there was a tiny breeze before a hurricane or tornado. *Oh no, not another mad rush of kids like the bus riders!* Soon a huge crowd of kids came storming down the hallway toward the gym. But it was different this time: Veer was prepared. As soon as the huge crowd hit him, he started weaving in and out. He still got bumped around, but at least he made it to the gym safely.

Once Veer entered the gym, he witnessed an amazing sight. Hundreds and hundreds of kids were filed into tight lines, with a minuscule path marked with cones cutting through the middle of the square. This was the largest group of kids Veer had ever seen at one place in his entire life. What seemed like an endless line of students was herded into the tiny gym, the teachers being the shepherds. The teachers directed the kids into the compact formations with no room to breathe. Veer was soon packed next to the worst possible people to sit next to, the eighth-grade bullies he had the pleasure of meeting earlier that day.

"Hey, look, Jed, it's that dweeb who didn't know what Sevy-Bop day was." The bully next to him, a stocky lump of an eighth grader named Gavin, laughed into Veer's ear.

"Yeah, that pathetic little coward who we almost knocked out in the hallway," Jed obnoxiously guffawed.

"Don't ever call me a coward," Veer mumbled. It wasn't that he was scared of bullies; he was just annoyed with them.

"What did you say, dweeb?" Jed yanked his collar as if he was trying to choke him. Just as the bully drew his fist back to aim a punch at Veer, a piercing screech echoed throughout the gymnasium.

Everyone immediately covered their ears to shield them from the deafening sound. Suddenly the piercing stopped and everyone looked up to see a tall thin man standing in the middle of the makeshift stage at the front of the gym. "Sorry about that. We're experiencing technical difficulties with the microphones this year." The man's low voice boomed throughout the gym. "Anyway without further ado, I welcome all rising seventh and eighth graders to the beginning-of-school assembly. My name is Mr. Thomas and I am the vice principal here at Medley Middle. We would like to start off our program with our new principal, Mr. Harrison."

There was a short round of applause after the vice principal's talk. Suddenly, a burst of laughter sounded as a short stocky bald man waddled up onto the stage. Sticking out from the back of his pants was a long tail of toilet paper dragging on the floor. "Excuse me, silence please, silence," the principal stated in a thick New York accent to interrupt the laughter. Still, stifled giggles were heard throughout the gym. *Is this a joke?* Veer thought to himself. But soon he learned it wasn't, as the vice principal bent down and whispered into the principal's ear. Veer couldn't help laughing to himself as he watched the principal's face turn from pale to beet red. The principal stood up on his toes to reach the microphone and stated in an embarrassed voice, "I have some matters to attend to, but I will be back shortly." With that, the principal did the closest thing to sprinting offstage that a stocky fifty-year-old could do.

The principal was back in less than thirty seconds, panting crazily with beads of sweat erupting from his forehead. His shoulders drooped as he forced his tiny legs up the stairs and onto the stage. "Students and teachers, I am Douglas Harrison, your new school principal. As the new principal, I have decided to host Medley Middle School's first annual Medley of Talents Competition." The principal paused, expecting applause, yet he was only met with sarcastic gasps of surprise. He continued, "This contest will test students in several aspects. The writing and math competitions will test students in academics. Students will be given a chance to showcase their musical talents in the music competition. An athletic competition will challenge students physically." Veer thought everything sounded good up until the athletics part; he wasn't so keen on that. "Groups are required to have three people, and to make things fair, there has to be at least one student from seventh grade and one from eighth. A single student from each group will compete in every competition. Also every group needs a teacher as a coach, and one teacher can coach three groups maximum. All students are required to compete." Groans were heard from all corners of the gym. The principal raised his stubby hand to signal silence. "You will receive all of this information on a form that your

5

homeroom teacher will give you. Fill out this form and pick your groups by next Monday or else you will receive an hour of detention for every day it is late."

"Can he seriously do that?" a scrawny pale kid with glasses asked Veer. Veer shrugged in response.

"Oh yeah, I almost forgot. There is a prize for winning each section of the whole Medley competition. The exact prizes haven't been decided upon yet, but I can tell you that they will be worth over a hundred dollars each." The principal chuckled.

"Now that's what I'm talking about," the scrawny kid yelled trying to attract attention.

This principal must be seriously into this competition, Veer thought to himself as the principal waddled offstage.

The next ten minutes seemed like an eternity as the vice principal discussed school procedures. Afterward, Ms. Bertha, a plump older lady huffed onto the stage. She went on and on in her high-pitched voice with the usual introduction to middle school spiel that Veer had heard at least a dozen times. He caught the usual catchphrases including "with freedom comes responsibility" and "don't be afraid make new friends." Just as Veer was nodding off to sleep, the bell cut Ms. Bertha off.

The sound of a thousand kids talking, yelling, and screaming exploded into Veer's ear, shaking him up from his drowsy state. Now it was time for Veer to head off to his first period class.

After picking up his books, which seemed to weigh at least two tons, from his old and rusty locker, Veer headed to the bathroom to wash up. Luckily, the bathroom was right next to his locker, so he left his books outside and headed in. His luck didn't last long, for this was the worst school bathroom Veer had seen in his life, and his old school's was pretty bad! Wet muddy paper towels were strewn across the cracked tile floor, the walls were dented, and the paint was peeling off. Veer tiptoed around the paper towels, holding his nose to block the reeking smell. Once he got the ancient faucet running, he splashed cool water on his face. He also looked in the full-length mirror to see if there were any scratches on his face from the trampling, or when the bullies almost beat him up. He looked into his own big dark brown eyes and at his tanned brown skin. He ran his eyes down his short scrawny body, his soft shortly-cut black hair, and his narrow face. It seemed to him that his ears stuck out too much and his face was too thin. At four feet six inches and seventy-five pounds as a twelve-year-old, it seemed like almost anyone could beat him up.

Why couldn't I be tall and strong like my cousins, or at least be average-sized like all my friends? How come I got all of the bad genes in my family? Veer thought to himself.

After drying his face off with the coarse school paper towels, Veer glanced at himself once again in the mirror and headed out the bathroom door.

As Veer was picking up his heavy load of books outside the bathroom door, he felt someone bump up into his shoulder. He looked up to see a familiar round face with big glasses.

"Oh, sorry, Veer," Vidya, one of his best friends, said in her characteristic bubbly voice. Vidya was Veer's nanny's daughter. He had pretty much grown up with her, as she had spent all of her holidays and summers with Veer's family. Veer considered Vidya his sister, and she could always bring a smile to Veer's face.

"Hey, Vidya, how's your first day going so far?" Veer replied. "Mine isn't going too well."

"Same here. I've already had five people call me you-know-what." She sighed. Ever since preschool, students had jeered at Vidya, calling her "four-eyes." She earned the nasty nickname because of her thick big glasses sitting atop her round nose. Even with today's technology, the ophthalmologists couldn't fix her poor eyesight. Instead of ignoring the years of taunting, like Veer did, Vidya had grown extremely sensitive to nicknames.

"Don't worry about it," Veer comforted his friend. "Everyone's strange on the first day of school." He glanced at the clock. "I'll catch you later because I'm almost late to first period."

"I guess I am too. Bye, Veer." Vidya waved. She briskly walked away, her long black ponytail swished side to side.

Veer remembered something about tardies and detention from Mr. Thomas's speech at the assembly, and picked up his books and ran to first period. His first class was science, and Veer didn't want to be late on the first day. He ran all the way from his locker upstairs, to Room 151, which was downstairs and at the opposite end of the school. He stepped into the room just as the ear-splitting bell rang and grabbed the only remaining seat, next to the scrawny kid sitting in front of him at the assembly.

"Hey! This seat is taken!" he yelled right into Veer's face.

"Sorry, but it's the only one left," Veer said as he scooted his stool away from the strange student.

"Why, I oughtta . . ." The kid tried to act like a tough guy. He pulled up his sleeve as to show his muscles, but all there was to show was a skinny pale arm.

"Oughtta do what, Greg? Cry to your mommy?" A kid behind Veer snickered. Before Greg could retaliate, the teacher's loud rough voice echoed through the large room.

"Hola, me llamo Profesor Coltz. Cómo están?" the tall teacher said in a proud voice. Everyone in the classroom looked at each other in confusion, waiting for someone brave enough to ask the teacher what he was talking about. *Is this guy lost?* Veer wondered to himself.

"Aren't you supposed to be teaching us science?" Greg yelled. "I mean, come on. I want to learn. Right, you guys?" He looked back expecting support. Instead he got a bunch of sleepy bored faces and a couple of snickering classmates.

"Oh, I thought I was teaching Spanish 1 this year," the teacher said in a Spanish accent with a concerned face. He was tall with combed dark hair and a short beard. After a couple of seconds, the worried frown turned into a mischievous grin. "Yes, I did it!" he proclaimed. "I knew I could trick you guys. I was just messing with you with all of that Spanish stuff and you bought it! I should be given an award for that." He laughed.

Veer sighed in relief. He was worried that he was stuck in the wrong class!

"Anyway, what I said in Spanish was 'Hello, I'm your teacher Mr. Coltz. How are you doing?'"

"Good," the class said in a monotone in unison.

"Geez. What are you guys, a bunch of drones? Come on, cheer up, it's the first day of school!" Mr. Coltz said sarcastically. "Something that will cheer you up is science this year!" With that, he presented to the class a slideshow about the "Upcoming Year in 7th Grade Science."

The slideshow had a bunch of interesting pictures of several fascinating topics that would be part of the curriculum. Veer and several other students were actually looking forward to science this year. He could already tell that Mr. Coltz wasn't a dull science teacher and wanted to make things exciting for his students.

After the slideshow was over, Mr. Coltz explained all the classroom rules, lab safety procedures, and the handling of equipment. Veer was happy to hear that Mr. Coltz wasn't using a textbook because textbooks made his backpack extremely heavy, and he would almost topple over whenever he put it on. Also Veer was glad when he heard Mr. Coltz say there wasn't going to be much homework this year. The class had given him a round of applause in gratitude when he stated this. Everybody but Greg had clapped because he said he liked homework, but he only did so to attract attention.

For the rest of the class period, Mr. Coltz talked about the outdoor activity the class was starting the next day. It involved rabbits, so many of the girls cooed "awww" and several boys smirked. Mr. Coltz thought it was funny and laughed about how his students did that every single year.

Veer was beginning to like Mr. Coltz more and more. *He's definitely going to be a popular coach for the Medley of Talents competition.* Veer made a note to himself to try extra hard to get Mr. Coltz as his coach.

The deafening bell interrupted Mr. Coltz's explanation of the outdoor activity. Students immediately got up and stampeded toward the door. "No homework tonight! Have an awesome first day!" he yelled above the din to the exiting students. Veer stayed behind to ask Mr. Coltz to be his coach, but he was too late. A bunch of other students had swarmed around the science teacher and Veer had no chance of getting through the ring of students asking for a coach. He had no time to spare, so he said a quick "bye," and ran to catch his next class.

Veer weaved through the crowded halls of Medley Middle. He rushed to his math class at the other end of the school in Room 208. He held his school map in one hand

and his pile of binders in the other as he walked between huddled groups of nervous students. At every corner, he quickly checked his map to see if he was going the right way. One time he almost turned the wrong corner, but he corrected himself and made it to math class just in time.

When Veer entered the room, there was absolute silence as the tall thin teacher sorted through papers at his desk. Veer grabbed a desk next to Vidya in the back of the room and didn't dare to break the silence. Veer knew the honors math teacher at Medley Middle, Mr. Steel, because his brother, Jai, had been in Mr. Steel's class the year before. Jai told Veer that Mr. Steel had an unconventional teaching style. He followed no curriculum and just loved math. Jai assured Veer that though Mr. Steel may appear mean at first, he was actually extremely nice. From his brother's experiences, Veer knew math would be fun this year.

After a couple of minutes, Mr. Steel got up stretched then started to speak in a matter-of-fact voice. "I guess I should give you guys a cute little speech about starting school. But, guess what? I'm not. This is an advanced math class, so we better start learning now. Right?"

Veer and Vidya exchanged glances, shrugged, and responded with a "right" as did the rest of the class.

"In this class, we are going to learn what even some graduate math students haven't learned about yet. No more of the elementary school math where you play with little yellow blocks." Stifled giggles were heard throughout the classroom. "All right, your test grades say you're smart, so I'm going to give you some pretty tough homework," he said as he passed out a sheet of three word problems. "If you can't get it in thirty minutes, don't go crying to your mommy . .

." Now students burst out in laughter. "I will explain the answers in class tomorrow," Mr. Steel continued. Mr. Steel began by jumping right into tough algebraic equations. Many students struggled to understand the difficult concepts, but Veer and Vidya were easily answering the complicated problems. Mr. Steel seemed impressed with them, but he didn't show it right away. The only other person able to answer Mr. Steel's complex questions was an intense-looking student, named Hal, sitting in the front of the classroom. Every single time Mr. Steel asked a question, his hand shot up and if Mr. Steel didn't call on him, he complained with a long groan. Though Veer loved math too, he didn't complain when he wasn't called on, unlike Hal. Vidya caught on to Hal's strange behavior as well, and made a questioning gesture at Veer. Veer just shrugged in response.

Once Mr. Steel finished his lesson, he handed out a worksheet with twenty equations scribbled in messy handwriting. Veer quickly finished up the work sheet with five minutes left in class. In his downtime, he noticed the interesting signs and pictures posted around the room. Some had pi written in large bold letters while others had various scientific formulas printed in a colorful decorative font. As Veer was trying to count how many digits of pi were on a certain sign, the loud bell rang. He jumped out of his seat and ran out of the doorway, on his way to music class.

Veer waved bye to Vidya and scurried around clusters of students on his way to Room 132. As Veer ran to his locker upstairs to deposit his huge pile of books, he accidentally bumped into the overly enthusiastic student from Mr. Steel's class, Hal. Hal was only slightly taller than Veer. He had bushy brown hair and a constantly furrowed brow.

"Jeez, what's your problem? Stop bumping into me you jerk!" Hal screamed into Veer's face.

"Sorry, but just take it easy, man." Veer tried to calm Hal.

"I don't have to listen to you, idiot," Hal retorted, and then walked away.

Why does that kid get worked up over the smallest things? Veer wondered as he ran up the stairs. He raced to his locker then carefully twisted the dial to his combination. Veer tried to pull the handle and open up the locker, but the old rusty door wouldn't budge. He tried his combination a second and third time, but to no avail. Finally, on his fourth try, the rusty hinges creaked open and Veer tore open his locker. Knowing he was going to be late, he quickly stuffed his books inside the tiny compartment, pulled out his music folder, and ran down the hall.

Running to every class is really getting old. Five minutes to get from classroom to classroom isn't enough, Veer thought as he jumped down the stairs, expecting to hear the bell any second. And sure enough, it rang loud and clear as Veer sped down the hallway to the music classroom.

As he entered the large spacious music room, Veer expected to find a young excited music teacher, like the one he had at his old school. But he was unpleasantly surprised to find Ms. Bertha, the old lady from the assembly, waiting for him with a stern expression and a menacing red tardy slip.

CHAPTER 2

On the afternoon of the next day, Veer stepped up the muddy steps and onto his rickety old yellow school bus, his thoughts clouded by the constant din of students' anxious voices. He hunched over, supporting his unbearably heavy backpack, while he waddled through the skinny aisle of the small bus looking for an open seat. Veer noticed that all of the seats in the front were taken, so he was forced to sit in the back, near the rowdy eighth graders.

Veer picked a tattered brown leather seat that was the closest to the front of the bus that he could get. Just as he was setting down his stuffed backpack, Veer heard a familiar voice jeering at him. "Hey, Jed, it's that little pipsqueak that we saw at the assembly." Veer turned around to see the chubby eighth-grade bully Gavin making faces at him.

"Oh yeah, that kid who we almost knocked out with that Sevy Bop Day prank!" Jed laughed as the two high-fived each other. *Just great! Now I have to deal with them on the bus too!* Veer thought to himself.

"Stop making fun of my little brother!" Veer heard his brother say from behind him. Veer found his older brother, Jai, standing next to him defending him from the annoying bullies.

"Like you can do anything about it, Jai. You're as much of a pathetic little punk as your baby brother is," Jed said in a sour voice.

"We aren't punks." Jai stood up to the aggravating bully.

"Whatever, dork," Jed said sarcastically as he rolled his eyes.

Just as Veer was about to retaliate, Jai put his hand in front of Veer in order to stop him. "They're not worth fighting," Jai whispered to his little brother. Veer listened to Jai and nodded a "thanks" as he watched his skinny older brother walk farther to the back to sit with some of his eighth-grade friends.

Though sometimes he can be a bit annoying, Jai is pretty cool sometimes, Veer thought as he settled into his seat. It was not long before Veer spotted Vidya stepping on to the bus. She walked through the skinny aisle and sat in the unoccupied seat next to Veer.

"Hi, Veer!" Vidya greeted her friend with a cheerful smile.

"Hey, Vidya, how was your second day?"

"It was better than the first. Most of my teachers seem decent, and I loved my art teacher, Ms. Easel. I'm thinking of asking her to coach me for the Medley-of-Talents."

"Your day was definitely better than mine. My shop teacher is the grumpiest guy I've ever seen. Also gym is as horrible as I expected. My gym teacher is hyper and wants us to get started with physical fitness testing, the nastiest part of gym, next week. And the worst part of it all is that gym is seventh period, which means I have the most awful class at the end of the day."

"That's pretty harsh," Vidya agreed with Veer. "My gym schedule isn't the greatest either, I have it first period.

But I guess we just have to live with it." Vidya shrugged. This was another example of what always surprised Veer about Vidya. She never felt down or sad and always was her optimistic self even in the harshest circumstances.

"Well, I better go and sit up front with Janice. I promised I would help her with her math homework today."

"Okay. See you at the bus stop." Veer watched his friend move toward the front of the bus. Soon Veer saw a familiar small figure walking toward the bus. As the figure approached, Veer recognized the freckly face of his elementary school pal, Brian. When Brian was new to school, Veer defended him from two bullies that were trying to take his lunch money. Ever since, they had been good buddies.

"Sup, Veer," Brian greeted Veer as he sat down in Vidya's old seat.

"Hey, man. It's awesome that we have two classes together," Veer responded.

"Yeah, I'm looking forward to shop and gym this year."

The loud roaring of the bus engines interrupted their conversation. The entire bus started to shake as black smoke started spewing out of the exhaust pipes. *Man, this bus is messed up,* Veer thought as the ancient vehicle chugged out of the school parking lot. The worst part of it all was that Veer would have to spend lots of time inside of the rusty old bus because he was the first stop to get on in the morning, and the very last stop to get off in the afternoon.

The rest of the bus ride was fairly uneventful. Jed and Gavin tried to annoy Veer by poking at him through a small hole in the beat-up seat, but Veer just ignored them. One by one, students trickled off the bus until Veer, Vidya, and Jai were the only people left.

The bus finally screeched to a halt, and the shutter doors flew open. Veer put on his heavy backpack and walked up the aisle and down the stairs to join Jai and Vidya outside. Veer found himself exiting the rusty old bus to meet a dreary rainy day outside. The trio watched the yellow bus slowly drive away before heading on their way to Veer and Jai's house.

As Veer, Vidya, and Jai sauntered home, they noticed how summer was fading away. No longer was the sun gleaming brightly, lighting the vast yards of large houses in the neighborhood. Now gray clouds were the only things to be seen in the sky, threatening to let rain pour at any moment. Brittle leaves crunched under their feet as the trio walked along the long meandering sidewalk approaching Veer and Jai's house. Fall always made Veer depressed.

Soon Veer and Jai's colossal house came into view. The giant mansion was spread over five acres of land and was a work of beauty. Intricate bronze patterning covered the windowsills and the top of the elegant mahogany double doors. The roof was covered with magnificent tiles, each with unique details. A wide perfectly trimmed lawn covered the long expanse in front of the house. Cutting through the front yard was a long smoothly paved driveway. Veer and Jai's house was truly a piece of art.

But Veer could no longer truly appreciate the beauty of his house, because inside he felt a great emptiness. He could sense Jai had the same cold and heavy feeling as they strode down the lengthy driveway toward their home. Vidya, on the other hand, was chattering endlessly about the coming of fall and the breathtaking sight of the colorful leaves on the grand trees surrounding the house. Normally, Veer and Jai would have enjoyed Vidya's light-hearted comments, but today was different.

"Vidya, how can you speak about the beauty of fall today of all days?" Jai interrupted Vidya in a sullen voice.

"C'mon, Jai, give her a break. She's only trying to cheer us up," Veer defended.

"Well, it's not working," Jai retorted.

A long sad silence followed. None of the three friends wanted to talk about the obvious, what everyone in Veer's household was very emotional about. But they knew someone would have to bring it up sometime that day.

Rain had just started to drizzle as the trio reached the intricate stone sidewalk leading to the grand mahogany double doors. The friends rushed to the door to escape the rain and rang the doorbell repeatedly. Veer peered through the window to see Anu Reddy, Vidya's mom, hurrying toward the door. Anu had been Veer and Jai's nanny since they were toddlers, and they both affectionately called her *Mousi* (aunt).

The mahogany doors finally swung open. A warm happy face greeted them with a friendly smile. "Hey, guys! How was your second day?" Anu said in a loving, but sad, voice with the slightest hint of an Indian accent.

Veer and Jai didn't reply. Their faces were pale with sorrow as they stepped through the front door. "It wasn't the greatest, but it wasn't horrible, Ma," Vidya responded.

"Well let me make you guys a fresh hot snack," Anu said, obviously trying to cheer them up. With that, she hurried over to the kitchen to gather all of the ingredients she needed to fix their meal.

"Come on, guys!" Vidya beckoned her friends toward the kitchen. The two brothers followed her in silence, not responding. *This is the closest I have seen them to shedding a tear since when it happened, exactly a year ago . . .*

"Vidya, I need help!" Her mother's call from the kitchen interrupted her thoughts. Vidya rushed over to the kitchen to aid her mother. "Can you help me chop these potatoes?" her mother said as she bustled about the kitchen finding vegetables, various spices, and other ingredients for a delectable classic Indian snack, samosa. As Vidya chopped the potatoes, she watched her friends as they sat solemnly, their faces stricken with sorrow. "Vidya, are you done with those potatoes yet? We need to simmer all of the vegetables in the spices." Once again her mother's voice snapped her out of her train of thought.

"Yes, Ma," Vidya loaded the chopped potatoes with the peas in the frying pan while keeping an eye on Veer and Jai for any sign of movement. They sat frozen in the same position at the kitchen table, not moving a muscle. As the vegetables simmered, Vidya and her mother began to roll out the pastry dough that the vegetables would sit in. They gathered the soft warm mixture of flour, butter, and salt that Anu had mixed earlier that day. They began to flatten the thick balls of dough by using rolling pins. Once they finished, they had to let the vegetables cool for a couple of minutes.

"Hey, Ma, shouldn't we try to console Veer and Jai?" Vidya asked her mother in a hushed anxious voice.

"No. We should just try to act as lively as possible to cheer them up. We should let them reflect with their mother as soon as she gets home. We shouldn't make their mournful day worse. Besides, we have to finish making these samosas," her mother replied. With that, they began to shape the flat dough circles into cones. Then they filled the cones with the cooked vegetables. Finally, they sealed each bundle one by one and deep-fried them. All the while, Vidya watched Veer and Jai, starting to feel their pain.

Their loss had also affected her just as much, for she had grown up with them, almost part of their family. Soon the samosa were finished frying, and Vidya loaded the scrumptious triangle-shaped snacks onto a large serving plate with the help of her mother and transferred the plate over to the dinner table.

Expecting Veer and Jai to delve into the plate as they usually did, she was surprised when they barely even showed any interest when she brought them to the table.

"C'mon, guys, why don't you have at least one samosa?" Anu pleaded with the siblings.

"We're not hungry," Jai whispered in a shaky voice.

Vidya shot a quick worried glance at her mother. The two brothers didn't move an inch, and their faces remained in the same stone cold expression. When Vidya looked back to her mother for reassurance, she was shocked to see something that she had never seen before in her life. Her mother actually looked *scared*. Vidya's mother had always been the one aiding everyone, helping them along and consoling them, and she was always brimming with confidence. But for the first time ever, her mother was frightened and utterly devastated. Vidya couldn't blame her; this tragedy had affected and changed anyone close to Veer's family.

Just when Vidya thought the tension was going to snap and someone was going to break down into tears, the doorbell rang. "I'll get it," Anu called as she hurried through the foyer toward the front door. Vidya heard the door swing open and her mother say "Hi, Jyothi!" as she greeted Veer and Jai's *amma* (mother).

"Hi, Anu," Veer heard his amma say in a pleasant voice, but Veer could tell she was hiding her true feelings. Ever since Veer and Jai's *nanna* (father), Samir Gupta, had suddenly and mysteriously disappeared exactly a year ago, Jyothi had been distant and solemn. Their nanna's disappearance had also worsened her medical condition. She had always been extremely frail and fragile. But with this devastating loss, it seemed as if she could faint at any second. Nevertheless, she had been a responsible and caring mother, always there to support her children whenever they needed assistance. Veer and Jai always knew that they could count on their mother, but on days like today, the one-year mark of their father's disappearance, they needed to support her as well.

"So, guys, how was your second day of school?" Jyothi asked as she strode into the kitchen, setting her large leather purse on the counter.

"It was fine, Amma. But I couldn't stop thinking about Nanna, and the day he just vanished," Veer responded.

"Same here," Jai echoed quietly. Another long silence followed.

Vidya was the first to speak, "I just can't believe someone as strong, intelligent, and resourceful as Uncle would just randomly disappear one day. It just doesn't seem possible."

"I agree with Vidya. Something has to be wrong. How could Nanna vanish so suddenly?" Jai wondered.

"I remember that day so clearly," Veer reminisced. "Nanna was in such a rush to go to Medley Middle School for some odd reason."

"Oh yeah, he went to drop off some things for the Medley of Talents competition," Jai remembered.

"During that entire year before he disappeared, he was so involved in organizing that Medley of Talents competition. He was so excited to have you guys join in and have fun competing," Jyothi reflected.

"Yeah, but why did he need to drop off the items to the school so urgently?" Vidya pondered.

"He never returned that day, and he's been missing since. Even after the police searched our house and the entire local area, nobody had reported seeing him since," Jai added in a shaky voice.

"I also remember that for weeks after Nanna's disappearance, Jai, Vidya, and I thought we saw people sneaking around our house," Veer said.

"We would always see the same man wearing sunglasses and a suit, but once we ran outside to check things out, he would be gone," Jai said.

"I think I also saw a tall lady with an overcoat in the backyard," Vidya added. "But I just thought it was my eyes playing tricks on me," she said as she shifted her thick glasses.

"I can't believe that the police already closed the case even after we told them about our suspicions. They had no explanation for all those people snooping around our house." Jai's grief was beginning to turn into anger.

"I for one, think those people may have had something to do with your dad's disappearance. They didn't seem friendly, and they looked suspicious, judging from what you guys described," Anu said confidently.

"It's possible that they could have taken him captive, but then there is no point in sneaking around our house. Things just don't make any sense," Veer stated.

"Well he was always a technology genius." Besides his job as a surgeon, and being a loving father, Samir spent any free time exploring technology. "Maybe they took him captive to force him to do some sort of special job for them," Vidya proposed.

"Maybe. But I have a feeling that it had to do with his career. He was such a talented and renowned surgeon; anyone could have wanted his medical expertise, but perhaps for the wrong reason," Anu said.

"But we're not sure who these people are, let alone if they took Samir. After all they could have just been visiting our new neighbors," Jyothi posed.

"But that wouldn't explain them sneaking around our house!" Veer proclaimed.

"Even if they did capture him, how could they do it in broad daylight?" Vidya brought up a good point.

"They could have taken advantage of his poor hearing in some way," Veer wondered out loud.

"But his hardness of hearing hadn't ever hampered Nanna and it never will," Jai said.

"Well I think something is wrong, and it takes three bright young minds like yours to figure it out." Anu looked at the three children lovingly.

"It just bothers me so much that no one was able to trace him anywhere even with all of the current tracking technology." Vidya sounded puzzled.

"We have had this conversation over and over, but we still can't seem to resolve anything," Jyothi said in a sad and disappointed voice.

"We've just got to find him, I know he is out there somewhere!" Veer stated in a determined voice.

"I say that we just keep on the lookout for anything strange that has remotely to do with Nanna's disappearance," Jai said.

"Yeah, I say we start with our school, because strangely enough, that's the last place we know he went before he vanished," Vidya suggested.

"All right, we should try to meet at school to share all of our findings," Veer said.

"Okay, agreed," Jai and Vidya responded. With that resolution in mind, Veer and Jai delved into the samosas. They had a new sense of purpose.

CHAPTER 3

Veer woke up to a soft scratching sound at his windowsill. Thinking it was just a bird, he shifted sleepily to his side to see what time it was. He glanced at the neon green numbers of his alarm clock that showed 5:50 AM. Glancing around the calming blue scene of his bedroom before closing his eyes one more time to catch ten minutes of sleep before school, he thought he spotted a shadow near his windowsill. Once again, a scratching sound came from his window. But this time around, it was louder, and he thought he heard somebody grunt with fatigue. Now he was suddenly awake. He jumped out of his bed and rushed over to the window to confirm his suspicions. But once he tore open the curtains, all he saw was the familiar scene of his beautiful front yard, with the colored fall leaves blowing in the wind. He glanced down to see if anyone could have possibly climbed the wall leading to his room. For a second he thought he saw a figure in the bushes, though he was sure his sleepy eyes were playing tricks on him. With a groggy sigh, he closed his curtains and started to get ready for school.

Then he remembered the resolution that everyone had agreed upon, and for the first time since Samir had disappeared a year ago, Veer was actually excited and anxious to get to school to look for clues. Though soon his happiness faded as he remembered what was looming upon them the next day. Tomorrow was going to be one of the most dreaded days of the school year, for it was time for physical fitness testing.

With both the dismay of having to face physical fitness testing and the excitement of finding clues in mind, Veer exited his room and started to walk sleepily down the steps. Once at the table, he found Jai half-asleep with an untouched muffin in front of him. Veer took a muffin and started nibbling, trying to keep himself awake. Fortunately, Veer looked at the time when he was halfway through finishing his muffin. He and Jai were already five minutes late. Veer quickly aroused Jai with a tap on the shoulder, and the two brothers raced to the foyer. They said a quick bye to their amma, as she too was leaving for work, and ran out the front door.

Veer and Jai sprinted down their long driveway and to the sidewalk, trying to stop themselves from toppling over from the huge weight of their backpacks slowing them down. Once they reached the sidewalk, they turned to run uphill to the street corner, where they could spot Vidya from a distance, waiting for the bus to come. Thankfully, they hadn't missed their bus, though they could hear it rumbling in the distance. Still struggling, the two brothers barely made it to the bus stop in time. Veer and Jai were both heavily panting, though Jai had an even tougher time with his asthma. He was wheezing and coughing all the while. Slowly, Veer and Jai climbed up the stairs of the rusty old bus and took their seats for a long bus ride to school.

Relieved to have made it on time, Veer looked around the nearly empty bus to find Vidya sitting in the seat next to him. Though Veer was unfortunately the first stop to get on and the last stop to get off, there was one benefit: he had the flexibility of sitting anywhere he wanted in the morning. He took advantage of his opportunity and distanced himself from the back where Jed and Gavin, the two bullies, were going to sit.

"Aren't you excited about finally looking for some clues related to your nanna's disappearance?" Vidya asked in a cheery voice.

"Yeah!" Veer said excitedly. "But we have physical fitness testing tomorrow, and I'm definitely not looking forward to that," he continued, sounding anxious.

"Yeah, me too," Vidya said with a dismayed sigh. "But we'll get it over with soon enough, and we have the Medley of Talents competition to look forward too."

"Oh yeah, the team rosters are due by Monday. I haven't gotten a team yet, have you?" Veer asked.

"No, I'm not on a team yet. And I haven't even asked for a teacher to mentor me either. We only have today, tomorrow, and the weekend to get everything together, so I say we both get started soon," Vidya responded in a worried voice.

The screeching of the bus to a shuddering stop interrupted the two friends' conversation. Veer was dismayed to find Jed and Gavin snickering as they jumped up and into the bus. With them was a tall lanky dark-skinned boy wearing a vest and torn jeans with short spiky black hair colored with blond highlights. He appeared to be joining in on the snickering and jeering, obviously a newfound friend of Jed and Gavin.

As the three bullies approached Veer and Vidya, the guffawing increased as they started to point and laugh at

Veer. "How do you like the new addition, pipsqueak?" Jed said as he casually punched Veer in the nose.

"Yeah, his name is Sid. He's our *favorite* sevy," Gavin snickered.

"He's going to be in our Medley of Talents group. We are goin' to wipe the floor with your pathetic little club of nerds. Aren't we, Sid?"

Sid contorted his face into what looked like a smile and nodded. As the band of bullies moved to the back to tantalize other bus riders, Sid shifted his backpack to the side and once he moved past Veer, he sharply pivoted, allowing the full weight of his backpack to strike Veer across the face. The sheer power of the blow caused Veer to be shoved against the back of his seat, leaving a large bruise on his cheek. Searing pain shot through Veer's face as he looked back to see Sid flash a sinister grin. The bully then sat down in the seat adjacent to Jed and Gavin and started guffawing at jokes that Veer had a feeling were pointed at him.

"Just ignore them; they'll never win Medley of Talents with three annoying bullies like them on their team," Vidya pointed out.

"Yeah, I know, but they really get on my nerves! Even though it will never happen, I would love to beat them at one of the physical challenges of Medley of Talents!" Veer retorted, hot with anger.

Vidya nodded in agreement just as the old bus screeched to a halt before Medley Middle School. Bus riders jumped out of their seats and sprinted out of the bus, and of course, the trio of bullies were the first ones off, pushing and shoving their way through the isle. Veer and Vidya patiently waited until they got in line right after Jai, and soon the three friends exited the bus as well. Just as Veer started to head toward the main entrance of the school, he thought he saw a flicker of movement on the school roof. Though when he blinked, all he saw was a patch of blue sky. *This is the second time my mind is playing tricks on me today. Is it just a coincidence?* he wondered as he rushed toward his locker, trying to make it to first period on time.

Veer sprinted into Mr. Coltz's classroom with only a few seconds to spare. Throughout the period, he was alert for any odd signs that may have led him to believe that all of the strange happenings this morning weren't just a coincidence. But even after constantly keeping an eye out for anything out of place, Veer found no signs of such sort. He was surprised to find himself disappointed because of the lack of strange signs; he felt a thirst for adventure and excitement. Just as Veer was starting to feel down, he walked into math class to see another flicker of movement outside the window. But this time he was able to catch a glimpse of a mysterious figure. All he could make out was that the figure was wearing a black trench coat with sunglasses shielding the eyes. *Why would someone with clothing like that be lurking around our school? Was it the same person that was making noises near his window that morning and darting around the rooftop?*

Veer excitedly hurried over to tell Vidya his observations, though just as he was making his way toward her seat, the bell rang. Veer quickly put down his books and sat in his seat, his mind still pondering the mysterious figure in the trench coat. As the class period passed by, Veer could not take his mind off the strange happenings that occurred that morning.

"Veer, what is the square root of negative 4?" Mr. Steel asked.

Veer, taken off-guard because of his daydreaming, paused for a few seconds. "Ummmm . . . it's imaginary," he stated in unsure voice.

The rest of the class except Vidya and Hal laughed, thinking that Veer was making his answer up. "Actually, that is correct," Mr. Steel said in a low, but surprised voice after the laughter died down. Veer slipped back into his thoughts of the mysterious figure as Mr. Steel explained imaginary numbers. His train of thought was interrupted once again as the loud bell rang.

As Veer and Vidya exited the classroom, Veer began to excitedly explain the strange occurrences to his friend. Vidya looked taken aback when Veer told her about the mysterious figure in the trench coat. When she was just about to explain why she was surprised, her art teacher Ms. Easel pulled her aside to tell her about an honors program. "I'll tell you at lunch," she said to Veer as she walked toward her teacher.

Soon his suspicious thoughts vaporized as he remembered that he could not risk being late to Ms. Bertha's music class once again. He quickly rushed to his locker and headed toward the music classroom for another tedious hour of Ms. Bertha's lectures.

Veer entered the cafeteria to hear the loud raucous chattering student voices as well as the shouts of disgruntled teachers scolding misbehaved students. As he headed toward his lunch table to brag to his friends about the delicious lunch his mousi had packed for him, he remembered Vidya's promise to tell him her thoughts about the mysterious figure. He tried to spot her among the sea of students entering the cafeteria, but couldn't see the familiar face with large glasses. When he went to check the seat where Vidya usually sat, he was even more surprised to find the seat vacant. *Huh, that's strange. Vidya has sat here every day since school started.*

He began to sit down when he felt an extreme itching sensation on his arm. He slowly rubbed his bicep, trying to ignore the strange feeling, as he started to open his delectable lunch of Indian butter chicken. A second later, the itching on his arm rose to a level that he could no longer ignore, and the feeling would not subside. He quickly ran to the nearest bathroom, which was outside of the cafeteria, bumping into a few straggling students in the hallway. All the while, he could not help wondering where Vidya was.

Panting as he reached the bathroom, Veer looked around and was glad to see no other is present. He sprinted to the dingy, stained mirror to take a look at what was bothering him. Veer lifted up his T-shirt sleeve to get a better look at the source of his itching. On the exact spot that was itching, several large red bumps had sprouted out of the skin on his bicep. *I'm sure those were not there this morning. How could have they appeared so suddenly?* Not risking the unpleasant itchy wait until he could see a doctor, Veer decided to go to the school nurse. Though he still questioned his own decision, wondering if this was important enough to take a trip to the notorious school nurse, Ms. Hertz, Veer found that his feet were already taking him to the nurse's office.

Veer became even more nervous when he found himself standing at the door to what several students' called the "torture chamber." With his arm still itching, Veer summoned an ample amount of courage, gulped, and knocked at the foreboding door. He winced as the door creaked open and almost wished he had just stayed in the cafeteria. His arm now itched furiously as he faced Ms.

Hertz, and as Veer expected, she looked nothing like the caring nurse at his elementary school. She was stocky, and had a strange resemblance to the school lunch lady.

"What seems to be the problem?" she asked in a low monotone, her cheeks jiggling.

"Umm, I have an extreme itch on my bicep, and many large red bumps have appeared, though they were not there this morning," Veer quickly mumbled. Ms. Hertz furrowed her eyebrows, and a large crease formed above her brow. Thinking she was angry, Veer thought Ms. Hertz was going to kick him out. Just as he turned to leave, she spoke again, though this time in a different tone.

"Wow, that's strange, I've already had two similar cases this morning, and I've never even seen this type of rash before," she muttered quietly to herself, very surprised. "Let me give you a quick check-up," she said, louder this time. Then she lifted her arm and gestured Veer inside the sterile white room.

The door shut loudly behind him and he headed toward the closest chair. As he began to sit down, he was surprised to see Vidya and Jai sitting in the chairs across from him. Puzzled, Veer wondered why his friend and brother were coincidentally in the nurse's office at the exact same time he was, though he was too baffled to ask. Luckily, he didn't have to for Jai and Vidya were thinking the same thing.

"Are you here because of an itchy rash?" Jai quickly asked before Veer could even sit down.

"How did you know?" Veer was astounded, though he suddenly remembered the nurse saying something about two other cases of the same rash. "Wait, do you have it too?" Veer asked before Jai could answer.

"Mmhm, I have a bunch of red bumps on my legs," Jai replied. "And so does Vidya, but she has it around her eyes." Before another word was said, Ms. Hertz walked toward Veer, donned her latex gloves, and began her checkup.

"When did the first symptoms of the rash appear?" Ms. Hertz asked in her monotone as she poked and prodded Veer's arm.

"During lunch, just before I came to the nurse's office."

"And let me guess, you saw strange red bumps and came running to me," Ms. Hertz said as if she had already heard the story before. *And she probably had,* Veer thought as he glanced over toward Vidya and Jai. *How could we all have the same bizarre rash on the same day, while no one else has it?* Veer wondered as Ms. Hertz continued her checkup.

Satisfied, Ms. Hertz finally stopped her examination of Veer's arm and came to the conclusion that Veer had been expecting. "Yep, you definitely have the same rash as those other two," Ms. Hertz said as she pointed toward Jai and Vidya. "Well, all I can do is rub some cleaning alcohol on it and give you a Band-Aid. You're going to have to see a specialist," she said in her monotone. *Wow, that was helpful.* Veer had to stop himself from muttering sarcastically aloud as the nurse supposedly treated his rash, though all she did was make it itchier. "Oh, and I forgot to tell you, guys, you all have to wait here for the rest of the school day so you won't spread the rash, in case it is contagious. Also, you cannot ride the bus, so you will have to arrange for someone to pick you up," the nurse said while putting on a fiendish grin, as if she enjoyed bothering children.

The three friends groaned as the nurse handed them the phone and strode to her desk at the opposite end of the room. "I'd better call my Ma. She can pick us up," Vidya said, already dialing the number. As Vidya explained their situation to Anu, Veer voiced his thoughts to his brother.

"How is it possible for all three of us to get the same rare rash, but no one else in the school to get it?" Veer asked his brother.

"Beats me," Jai replied. Then suddenly a thought flashed through his mind. "Hey, don't you remember when Nanna suddenly got that strange rash?"

"Oh yeah, he had large red bumps on his ears, just like our rash. I remember him having it for a month or so before he disappeared," Veer said.

"Do you think it's possible that we have the exact same rash?" Vidya speculated, having finished her conversation with her ma. The question left the three friends silent for a few minutes, wondering if this rash was a strange coincidence.

"Hey Vidya, what were you going to tell me during lunch about the strange figure?" Veer changed the topic minutes later.

"Oh yeah, you were telling me about a strange cloaked figure with sunglasses, right?" she asked and Veer nodded. "Your description sounds similar to the figure that I glimpsed lurking around your house right before Uncle disappeared. It could be a coincidence, but I doubt it."

"So you think this figure that Veer saw today is the same one that you saw a year ago before Nanna disappeared?" Jai asked.

"I think so," Vidya replied.

"So what does it mean? Do you think that this figure has something to do with Nanna's disappearance, and now they are coming for us too?" Jai wondered as the three children exchanged anxious glances.

"Instead of worrying, I say we think about this logically," Vidya said. "This figure was lurking around your home and our school, and may have had something to do with Uncle's disappearance. There has to be some connection between everything."

"Well, the only connection between Nanna and our school is that he helped plan the Medley of Talents," Veer stated.

"So you are saying that we can find out more about Nanna's disappearance, our rash, and this mysterious figure if we investigate Medley of Talents?" Jai asked skeptically.

"Well, there may be some clues or leads if we all find out how Nanna was involved in Medley of Talents," Veer defended.

"He's got a point," Vidya said as she shifted her large glasses. "This is our best and only known shot at finding an explanation for all of these weird occurrences."

"We may not have much time because whomever that mysterious figure is working for may be coming after us. So I say we start investigating the Medley of Talents right away," Veer said.

"Well, because we have to work quickly, the most efficient way for us to investigate the Medley of Talents is obviously to work together. And that means we should all be in the same group," Jai said logically.

"That is true," Vidya agreed. "And we do have at least one student from seventh grade and one from eighth, so our team fits the rules."

"Sounds good," Veer stated. "But there is one more problem that has to be dealt with. Who is going to be our coach?"

"I have already asked all of my favorite teachers, and all of them are already coaching three other teams," Jai said.

"It's the same for me," Vidya explained as she wiped her glasses.

"Yeah, same goes for me too," Veer added. "But actually we shouldn't look for our favorite teacher to be our coach, rather the one who would help us find out more about how Nanna was involved. Since we are trying to find an explanation for all of these strange happenings, and Nanna is the link between all of them, the person who would worked most closely with Nanna would be the most helpful."

"He has a point," Vidya agreed.

"So which teacher in this school would know the most about Nanna's involvement in the planning of Medley of Talents?" Jai wondered.

Suddenly Veer remembered Samir talking excitedly about his meetings with Mr. Harrison about Medley of Talents. "Actually the person who would know the most about Nanna's involvement in Medley of Talents isn't a teacher. He is our new principal, Mr. Harrison," Veer explained as he giggled, remembering the toilet paper incident earlier.

"Aww, man, I don't want that guy who takes bathroom breaks in the middle of assemblies, and then comes back with a trail of toilet paper behind him." Jai giggled.

"But Veer does have a point," Vidya said. "Now I remember that Uncle had weekly meetings with Mr. Harrison about planning the Medley of Talents."

"But can a principal, who isn't exactly a teacher, be our coach?" Jai asked.

"There is no harm in asking," Vidya said optimistically.

"Well, if we want to find an explanation to all of these strange occurrences, we'd better ask him," Veer said.

"I guess that settles it. We'll ask him tomorrow morning right before school," Jai continued.

After a long silent, itchy pause, Veer wondered how much longer they had to wait. Looking at his watch, he figured that they had an hour left in the dreaded "torture chamber" of Ms. Hertz.

"I say we get started now to save time, knowing that this mysterious figure and whomever he is working for may be coming after us. Also, this means we have to keep our work a secret," Veer said, breaking the silence. Both Jai and Vidya nodded in agreement. "So, we should all start pooling our knowledge about the Medley of Talents to see if we can come up with any leads."

"Well, I've heard from my teachers that there are going to be five different contests, testing students in all aspects, from academics to athletics," Vidya started off.

"Yeah, I think there are going to be two academic events: math and writing. And I also heard about a music event, though I don't know the details, I think it's going to be a contest to see which group can play the best song," Jai stated.

"I think the other two events both have to do with athletics. My gym teacher keeps droning on and on about how students should get in shape for a race and an arm-wrestling event," Veer said.

"We should also remember that we not only have to try to find clues, but we also should attempt to perform as well as possible, just as the other groups. You never know what the prizes will tell us," Jai said.

"Jai's right, and I have confidence that we can earn at least three of the prizes, in the academic and music events. As long as we work hard, we are talented enough to win those competitions," Veer said.

"Remember that Mr. Harrison said that only one student from each group can compete in any one contest. So, I think we should start deciding who competes in which contest," Vidya said.

"Well, since we are all advanced in math, but I am a year ahead of you guys, in Geometry. I would like to take the math event," Jai said, and the other two agreed.

"I have always enjoyed writing, ever since I was little. I would love to compete in the writing event," Vidya said. The two brothers were happy to let her take part in the writing event, which wasn't one of their favorite subjects.

"I guess I'll compete in the music event," Veer stammered as his face turned a sickly pale color.

"What's wrong?" Vidya asked in a concerned voice.

After a long pause, Veer gulped and spoke. "As soon as I realized that I was taking part in the music event, the memory of my nanna giving me a brand new guitar for my birthday flashed into my mind. And besides, I haven't even practiced since Nanna disappeared, which was over a year ago."

"Don't just give up; you have to practice to give us a shot at winning. Anyway, your guitar teacher said that you were the best student she has ever taught," Jai consoled his brother as he patted him on the back.

"I guess I can try." Veer sounded a little more confident.

A loud knock on the door of the "torture chamber" interrupted the trio's conversation. "May I come in?" Veer heard a familiar gruff New York accent.

"Have I got a choice?" Ms. Hertz grunted back grumpily and went back to her desk. Veer was surprised to see the short, stocky figure of Principal Harris rounding the corner.

"Are you three Veer Gupta, Jai Gupta, and Vidya Reddy?" the new principal pronounced the three Indian names with remarkable accuracy. *That's strange; I've never heard anyone who wasn't Indian pronounce our names that well,* Veer thought to himself. The three nodded in unison. "Are you three on the same Medley of Talents team, and have any of you asked a teacher to be your coach?" he asked.

"Yes, we are on the same team, and no, we have not asked for a coach yet." Jai was the first to respond.

"Perfect," the principal said cheerfully in his New York accent. "Because, guess what, you have the privilege of the school principal being your Medley of Talents coach!" he continued. Without waiting for a response, the principal quickly walked out of the room.

Veer was dumbstruck. *Was that just a coincidence that he asked us to be our coach just as we decided to ask him to coach us? Or do all of these strange occurrences happening on the same day have a link between each other? This day just becomes weirder and weirder.*

The trio climbed out of Anu's battered station wagon. After a long rough day at school, they were ready to go to Vidya's house to relax and have some of Anu's delectable Indian snacks.

They started down the street toward the apartment complex. All of them walked at a leisurely pace, enjoying the early autumn afternoon. Alongside them was the neighborhood park, which now was a gorgeous sight that seemed like it was from a painting. Bright sun shone through tall oaks onto a ground colored with an array of vibrantly colored fall leaves. This was one of the main aspects of the Washington DC area that Jai enjoyed. Though it was becoming a sprawling area with offices, houses, and malls, the beauty of nature was still present alongside the buildings. He just hoped that wouldn't change in the future with the population of the area growing exponentially.

As they continued sauntering along, Jai thought he heard a branch snap. *Was someone there?* His mind immediately jumped to the strange figures around the house when Samir disappeared. But he soon dismissed the thought as paranoid. *What would they want with us?*

But then he heard the crunching of leaves, gradually getting louder. Jai stole a furtive glance backward and saw a flash of black. When he looked closer, he was sure he saw a tall man in a trench coat and sunglasses hiding behind a tree. Somebody was definitely following them.

Jai casually turned toward Veer and Vidya, not wanting to show their follower that Jai had seen him. "Somebody is following us," he whispered. Both Vidya and Veer's immediate reaction was to turn around, but Jai grabbed them before they could do so. "Just act normal. If he knows that we saw him, he might try to capture us. Let's just continue on to Vidya's house and act like nothing happened," Jai said calmly. Veer was surprised at how his brother remained collected even in dire situations.

"What?" Vidya replied, surprised. "You want to lead him to our house? Then he can get us whenever he wants."

"Vidya is right," Veer agreed. "We've got to shake him off our backs."

Jai looked backward. Now the man was less than a hundred yards away. "He's getting closer," he said nervously. "Any idea of how to get rid of him?"

The man then came into plain view, walking quickly toward them. His pace gradually got faster, and he soon broke into a jog, then into a full-out sprint.

"Run!" Veer yelled.

The trio bolted toward the park as an immediate instinct. The foliage would provide temporary cover and confuse their pursuer. They sprinted as fast as they could through the piles of leaves. But their follower was much faster with his long strides that retained a breakneck pace. Jai started to feel his lungs burning, and he began to wheeze uncontrollably as he struggled to gulp in more air. Soon his lungs felt as if they were going to burst any second! With his severe asthma, he couldn't keep running much longer.

"Guys, he's gaining on us," Jai said between wheezes and coughs.

Veer instantly thought of a solution. "Let's hide in the dip! There's no way he'll find us."

The "dip" was a spot that Veer painfully discovered years ago shortly following their moving in to their house. While he and Jai were riding their bikes and exploring the neighborhood, Veer veered off toward the far edge of the park that bordered on an abandoned farmyard. Little did he know that separating the two was a narrow yet deep riverbed that was hidden by overgrown vegetation. Before he could stop himself, Veer rode head on into the trench and suffered a broken arm because of it. Until now, Veer was careful never to set foot toward the dip again.

But now they had no other choice. Their pursuer was now only a hundred feet away and quickly approaching. The trio immediately changed direction and headed toward the abandoned farm. Jai was beginning to feel woozy and lightheaded. He glanced backward and sighted a blurry image of the pursuer charging toward them. They wouldn't make it.

But soon the forest thinned and the farm came into view. Jai spotted the thin line of overgrown shrubbery in the distance that concealed the dip. Veer and Vidya, who were a few feet ahead, dove into the brush and fell farther down into the hole beneath. Jai drew in a deep raggedy breath and jumped.

He felt vines pulling at him and thorns piercing his skin as he fell. Jai hit the ground with a resounding thump, but luckily the foliage cushioned his fall. He felt Vidya and Veer next to him, but he couldn't even see their outlines. The overgrowth blocked out nearly all of the sun. Hopefully, their pursuer wouldn't find them, because if he did, they were blind and done for.

The trio soon heard footsteps overhead. The man had stopped right in front of the riverbed. He was so close that they could hear his quiet panting.

"I lost them," he said.

"What? How is that possible? You were closing in just a moment ago," an electronic sounding voice responded. It came from a walkie-talkie.

"I know, but they're just gone." He sounded extremely frustrated and confused.

"Well if you don't find Gupta's kids, you know the consequences."

"Wait, I think I've got something."

The man slowly approached the growth of weeds. Suddenly, a hand thrust through the wall of plants above. Jai held his breath, for he knew that the pursuer couldn't see them. As long as the trio didn't make a sound, they were safe.

No matter how much pain he felt pounding in his chest, Jai forced himself to not make a sound. After what seemed like a century, the man finally pulled his hand to the surface after failing to find them.

"Never mind. I just don't know where they went."

"Find them!" The voice was so forceful that the man fumbled the walkie-talkie. It fell back through the brush and landed just a few feet from where Jai was crouching. *Uh-oh.*

The man cursed under his breath. The trio heard him clambering through the bushes and a loud thud as the men fell to the riverbed. By the sound of his breathing, Jai could tell that the man was less than a yard away. One false move and the trio was caught.

The man groped at the packed earth below, searching for the walkie-talkie. The sound of the man's breathing became louder. Now he was only inches away! Jai shut his eyes and prayed that by some miracle the man would not find them. But it was too late. The man's hand brushed against Jai's shoe then clenched it with a tight grip.

Jai was just about to let out a yelp when a loud blaring noise broke the silence. The walkie-talkie sputtered back to life even after a long fall down.

"What just happened?"

The man released his grip upon Jai's foot and scrambled to where the walkie-talkie lay. "It's too dark down here, I can't see a thing. I'll give you a detailed report back at base."

After the man climbed back through the bushes above, Jai let out a sigh of relief. The trio waited silently in the ditch until they were sure that their pursuer had left.

"What was that about?" Vidya said as she struggled back up the side of the riverbed. "Who was he and why was he chasing us?"

This time, Jai, who could usually come up with a logical solution, was clueless. "I have no idea. All I can say is that we have to keep our eyes peeled."

CHAPTER 4

Veer groggily opened his eyes the next day, recalling the many strange events that occurred the day before: the strange figure, the rare rash, the principal asking them to be their Medley of Talents coach, and the chase through the park. Yesterday also yielded many breakthroughs about Samir's disappearance, giving him a surging feeling of hope inside. After quickly glancing at his alarm clock, which never seemed to sound an alarm when it was supposed to, Veer lazily tumbled out of bed. As he stood up, the gloomy feeling of despair swept over him. As his mind slowly expelled the feeling of sleep from his body, he remembered that today was going to be the most embarrassing day of the school year. Today, he would have to compete in physical fitness testing.

As he slowly carried out his morning routine, he remembered how he was counting down to this dreaded day since the beginning of the school year. After taking a quick shower, Veer got dressed and headed downstairs. As he walked toward the kitchen, he remembered physical fitness testing last year. He was especially dismayed about the pull-up test. He recalled how he felt so helpless hanging from the cold metal bar, barely able to pull himself up an inch, and unable to complete a single pull-up. When he jumped down, he heard the snickering and jeering of the school bullies, and the giggling of girls who thought he was weak. That had to be the most embarrassing experience of his entire life.

He shook the bad memories from his head as he walked into the kitchen. Veer was surprised to see Jai awake, sitting at the kitchen table, staring at his uneaten cereal. Usually Veer would walk in to find Jai asleep, but this was the very first time this school year he kept his eyes open during breakfast. *He's probably just as nervous about physical fitness testing as I am.*

After a long silence, during which Veer finished his cereal in a few hungry slurps, Jai finally spoke. "I'm going to do so badly on the mile. My asthma makes it impossible for me to run long distances without stopping to walk. Everybody's going to make fun of me, just like they did last year."

"At least you can do a pull-up," Veer replied grumpily. Looking at the clock, he said, "Let's head toward the bus stop. I don't want to cut it close, like yesterday, and have to run all the way." He picked up his huge, heavy backpack and headed toward the front door, with Jai close behind him. After saying bye to their amma, Veer and Jai exited their large house and walked toward the bus stop.

At the bus stop, they found Vidya vigorously polishing her large glasses. "I just can't get my glasses cleaned," she explained as she furiously rubbed a gray cloth against her large lenses. "Every time I put them on, I get blurry vision. Either they are dirty, or somehow my eyesight has become worse overnight, and I think the first explanation seems more reasonable," she muttered to herself as she continued her futile attempt to clean her glasses.

"That's strange," Veer proclaimed.

"I know." Vidya put on her glasses and blinked uneasily a couple of times. "I'll have to see the eye doctor. Unfortunately, my Ma couldn't get an appointment until late this afternoon, so I'll still have to go to school. Luckily, I'll still survive, because my vision is not extremely blurry, but I won't be able to read or write today," she continued.

"That's fine." Veer consoled her. "We don't have any big tests today, other than physical fitness testing, which doesn't require reading or writing."

Just as Veer finished his sentence, their rusty old school bus rattled, creaked, and groaned as it made its way up the steep hill. Finally, the yellow behemoth screeched to a stop, and the thin double doors swung open.

"I'm not too worried about physical fitness testing anyway. Even if I don't do the best, which usually happens, I can always raise my grade in gym," Vidya said as she climbed the stairs into the bus.

"But aren't you afraid of people making fun of you?" Veer asked as he made his way down the narrow aisle, squeezing through the seats as he lugged his huge backpack. Avoiding the usual seats of the troop of bullies, Sid, Gavin, and Jed, Veer sat toward the front, with Vidya in the seat adjacent to him.

"No one has ever teased me about it before. These things matter much more for guys than for girls," Vidya responded.

"Lucky for you," Veer muttered grumpily, as he watched the dreaded trio of bullies walk confidently down the aisle. Before he could say another word, Veer was bombarded with a volley of spitballs hitting his head and torso. Flicking off a spitball that had been buried in his hair, Veer turned around to see Sid, Gavin, and Jed leaning over their seats with straws protruding from their mouths. Not wanting to pick a fight, Veer ignored them and turned around. He had to restrain himself from kicking the three bullies every time he heard their snickering about how he was a coward.

"They're just annoying bullies. You did the right thing by ignoring them," Vidya spoke quietly.

After Veer cooled off, he spoke. "Jed and Gavin are bad enough, but that new Sid kid is the worst. He gets pure enjoyment out of annoying seventh graders, just like Jed and Gavin, but he is the same age as us. Even though it doesn't justify anything, Jed and Gavin are older than us. Sid thinks he has the right to do whatever he wants to other seventh graders."

"Actually, you're wrong," Vidya said, surprising Veer. "Unfortunately, Sid transferred to my gym class yesterday. I learned that his actual name was Siddhartha Setty. Also I overheard the teachers talking about how he was suspended, and nearly expelled, so many times that he had to be held back a year. So he actually should be an eighth grader, and he isn't the same age as us, but a year older."

The rickety old bus shuddered to a stop. Veer saw his old pal Brian quickly leap up the stairs into the bus. Bursting with energy, Brian padded speedily down the aisle and plopped down into the seat next to Veer.

"Hey man, aren't you psyched about physical fitness testing in gym today?" Brian said cheerfully. Though he was small, Brian was strong for his size and fast. He was the top performer in all of the fitness tests in his elementary school the year before.

"No, not really," Veer replied gloomily. "But I bet you'll be the best in every single event this time, just like last year."

"I'm not so sure about that. There will be some tough competition this year, especially that new kid

Sid. I heard he's been held back a year, so he'll have the physical strength of an eighth grader." As Brian finished his sentence, the old bus creaked to its final stop in front of Medley Middle. All of the students jumped out of their seats with their large backpacks, clogging the narrow aisle. Veer waited until the congestion of the aisle decreased as students hopped off the bus. Veer was the last student to step off the bus and walk into school.

The school day passed by slowly as Veer tensely anticipated the last period, gym, in which he would partake in physical fitness testing. Each minute during class seemed like an hour, as he imagined the embarrassment of not being able to do a single pull-up once again and the mocking faces of students as he jumped down from the pull-up bar. He was so fazed that in science, he almost mixed two chemicals that would have caused a dangerous reaction, but luckily his lab partner stopped him. Also, in math he incorrectly answered the easiest question, which had never happened to him before, and of course, Hal rubbed it in. By sixth period in history, he was so nervous that his legs were shaking. When the loud bell toned at the end of sixth period, he felt as if his entire lower body was made of lead, and he could barely draw himself across the hallway into the gym.

As soon as the bell sounded, Veer's gym teacher, Mr. Randolph, blew into his silver whistle, creating a loud high-pitched shrieking noise. "Gather, soldiers," he yelled, and the students immediately sprinted to face him. Mr. Randolph, a retired marine, ran the seventh-grade gym class like a boot camp. He was notorious for being quick to hand out detentions for the slightest hint of disobedience, and for this he was given the nickname "Sergeant Detention." Students cowered in his presence, and even the troublemakers obeyed his orders without hesitation.

Slightly trembling, Veer stood facing Mr. Randolph with an erect soldier-like posture, waiting for his orders. Walking down the line of students, Mr. Randolph looked each one directly in the eye, looking for a sign of weakness. When he came across Veer, he suddenly stopped and peered closer. He came so close to Veer's face, that Veer could smell the gym teacher's garlic breath.

"Are you nervous, son?" he demanded.

"Slightly," Veer mumbled back.

"What did you say?" he yelled.

"Sir, yes, sir." Veer talked louder.

"Good, you should be, because today is the best day in the entire school year for me, and the worst day for you." After that, he broke into a cruel laugh. Then suddenly, without warning, he yelled "Soldiers, positions!" The students scrambled to different stations in which they would perform their physical fitness tests. After barely waiting a second, Mr. Randolph shouted, "You know what to do. What are you waiting for? Get started!"

Veer watched some other students do the timed sit-up test as he waited in line to do the sprint. He was in such a daze that when it was his turn to sprint, he was still staring at other stations.

"Are you deaf, son?" his gym teacher yelled. "I blew my whistle five times. Complete your sprint test now while I'm in a nice mood or it's detention for you, buddy."

Veer quickly obeyed, and stepped to the line. As soon as the whistle blew, he quickly jumped off the line. When he landed, his left foot hit his right, knocking him off-balance and sending him sprawling to the floor. Quickly recovering, Veer heard the snickers and giggles of other students laughing at him. As soon as his right foot touched the floor, searing pain shot through his ankle. Veer then half-jogged, half-limped the rest of the sprint. When Mr. Randolph called out the time, as expected, Veer's score was dismal.

With more snickering and giggling after Mr. Randolph called out his time, Veer hung his head down as he headed to his next station, dismayed about his sprint time. As soon as he reached the sit-up station, he saw his friend Brian finishing up his fitness test with ease.

"Hey, Veer, don't worry about it, man, your fall was just an honest mistake. Besides, you have four more tests to prove yourself," Brian called out as he quickly headed toward his next station. *All four in which I have the pleasure of having the worst score in the class,* Veer thought to himself.

Once again, Veer did not do well in his fitness test. Grunting and panting with exertion by his twentieth sit-up, Veer was forced to stop due to fatigue seconds later. With still half of a minute left, Veer tried to complete another sit-up, but as soon as he lifted his head off the ground, pain shot through his abdomen. It felt as if claws were ripping through his stomach every time he moved. Though it seemed like his muscles were screaming for him to stop, Veer forced himself to complete another sit-up in the last twenty seconds. All the while Mr. Randolph was screaming in his ear that he was weak, not helping Veer a bit. Massaging his abdominal muscles, Veer stood up and headed wearily to the next station.

After completing the flexibility test and the grueling mile run (in which he had to stop to walk several times), Veer walked into the center of the gym. Every muscle in his body was aching. Lining up to face the cruel gym teacher, beads of sweat poured down Veer's face. Strutting down the line of students, Mr. Randolph yelled out "Are you tired, soldiers?"

"Sir, yes, sir!" the students responded.

"Well too bad," he jeered. "Because I saved the best fitness test for last. Now we are going to do my personal favorite, the pull-up test!" Veer shuddered as memories from last year's pull-up test flashed back into mind. "Everyone to the pull-up bar!"

Waiting at the back of the mass of students in front of the pull-up bar, Veer did not want to be the first to do his pull-ups, if he could do any. Mr. Randolph was known to be the worst pull-up test proctor in the state. Ever since he set the Medley school record for pull-ups, completing twenty-seven when he was in seventh grade over forty years ago, he'd been bossing around kids who weren't strong enough to do many pull-ups. One time he gave a kid a week of detention just for not being able to do a pull-up. All Veer could do was just hope he wasn't the first in line to face his brutal gym teacher.

Shifting through the papers that contained the scores of students from their past years to decide which order the students would complete their fitness test, Mr. Randolph suddenly stopped and peered at one paper. *Please let this paper not be mine.* Veer hoped. Putting on a fiendish grin, Mr. Randolph called out. "First up to complete his pull-up test, Veer Gupta!" he yelled, horribly mispronouncing Veer's name. *Just great,* Veer thought to himself as he pushed and shoved his way to the front of the crowd of students. "It looks like you've got a bunch of *O*s on your paper," Mr. Randolph said as Veer approached the menacing pull-up bar. "Does that stand for outstanding? No, I don't think so. I think that's just the number zero, for the number of times you did a pull-up," he said mockingly. "Now hurry up with your pitiful attempt to complete a pull-up so I can give you two weeks of detention when you fail to do a single pull-up once again."

Reaching up and wrapping his hands around the cold metal bar, Veer closed his eyes and anticipated the embarrassment of the moment to come. In the background, he heard Mr. Randolph's piercing whistle as a signal to start the test. Adjusting his grip so he had a firm hold on the bar, Veer hoisted himself off the ground. *My body feels as light as a feather!* Easily Veer pulled his body so that his chin was way above the pull-up bar, then let his body drop back down. *Yes, my first pull-up!* Again and again, Veer did pull-up after pull-up, his sinewy biceps pumping up and down, until he fell into a rhythm. *It seems like there's no gravity and I'm weightless. There's nothing holding me back!* Before long Veer reached twenty-eight pull-ups, breaking the school record, and his friend Brian cheered him on. Everyone else, including Mr. Randolph, was too surprised to make a sound, though a clattering noise was made when Mr. Randolph's whistle fell from his gaping mouth and hit the floor. Soon Veer struggled more with each successive pull-up, his body feeling heavier and heavier as his arms became worn-out. Soon his arms were exhausted, and he strained to finish one last pull-up. He let himself fall back to the ground after thirty-two pull-ups, tired but elated. As time wore on when he watched others perform the fitness test, the euphoria of his accomplishment began to fade from his mind, and other thoughts quickly rushed into his head. *How is it possible for me to get strong enough all of a sudden to go from a pitiful zero pull-ups to a champion record of thirty-two?*

Jai's stomach felt uneasy as he walked out of the gym and onto the outdoor track where he would partake in the mile run. Thoughts from last year's physical fitness day when he ran the mile flooded his mind. He remembered that as soon as he started to jog, students breezed past him, and he soon fell to the back of the group. He immediately was filled with the gloomy sense of failure as he recalled having to stop and walk after a half lap into the run. His severe asthma caused him to cough and wheeze with extended physical exertion. That year, he had to walk most of the mile with his inhaler in hand, earning him the worst time in the class: fifteen minutes and forty-seven seconds. *I just hope that I can survive this year without an asthma attack,* Jai thought to himself as he patted his inhaler, which was always handy in his back pocket.

Jai looked down at his beaten-up running shoes as he positioned himself at the starting line. As he waited for the sound of the gym teacher's whistle signaling the start of the race, he heard someone snicker about his horrible mile time from last year. Jai's face flushed red with anger. *It is bad enough to have asthma and not be able to do any long-distance running. It's just wrong for someone to make fun of me for it.*

Jai's anger faded and was replaced by anxiety as he heard the gym teacher yelling "On your mark." Jai trembled as he positioned himself into the runner's stance. "Get set!" He gulped as he heard the sound of his gym teacher's gruff voice. Then a second later, the piercing high-pitch noise of the whistle signaled the beginning of the mile run.

As soon as Jai heard the sound of the whistle, he exploded off the starting line, sprinting to the head of the group. *Usually by this time, after taking more than ten strides, my asthma kicks in and I start to wheeze after each breath.* Jai took long, powerful strides and was speeding way ahead of the group. *How is this possible? I have no difficulty breathing whatsoever and I'm not even panting.* With each breath, Jai seemed to become faster and faster. By this time, Jai was already a half lap ahead of the second-place runner and expanding his lead every second.

Whizzing past the gym teacher, Jai couldn't help but smile when he heard his quarter-mile time of one minute flat and see the look of surprise on his gym teacher's face. Grinning, Jai pumped his legs more and more rapidly and lapped several runners. Jai had to stop himself from screaming for joy at the sensation of being able to move so quickly. Jai easily finished his second and third laps, his thin legs moving in a blur. By the fourth lap, Jai finally started to breathe harder. Drawing every last bit of reserve strength left inside of him, Jai completed his final lap. As soon as he rounded the bend, he sprinted the straightaway, his legs burning from exhaustion. As soon as Jai passed the gym teacher one last time, he collapsed on the soft grass and panted heavily.

"Five minutes flat!" Jai heard his gym teacher's brusque voice. Then in a slightly softer tone, she said, "Man, Jai, I didn't know you had it in you."

Panting and sweaty, Jai finally felt successful, filling in that vacant space of failure with the accomplishment of running the fastest mile this school had ever seen.

Vidya's stomach lurched as her ma's used decade-old red station wagon flew over a speed bump and into the parking lot of the optometrist's office.

"Sorry!" Anu said as the car swerved into the parking space and she slammed on the brakes. The two jumped out of the car, rushing because they were late to the appointment due to the notorious DC rush-hour traffic. Leaping up the steps and speeding toward the entrance to the optometrist's office, Vidya and Anu hurried inside.

They hastily made their way toward the front desk to greet an unprofessional secretary reading a gossip magazine and chewing gum. "How may I help you?" she said, not even caring to look up from her magazine.

"Vidya Reddy has an appointment at 3:30 to get her eyes checked," Anu responded.

Putting down her magazine, the secretary moved to her computer and typed lightning fast, her long fake pink fingernails a blur. "Mmhm, the appointment is confirmed," the secretary said as she quickly glanced up at Vidya. "Have a seat, and they will be with you shortly."

Sitting down on the beat-up blue chairs, Vidya looked around the room, but everything was blurry. Throughout the school day, everything seemed like a hazy blur. As soon as she finished up her physical fitness testing (which she performed poorly in as expected), Vidya couldn't take part in any of her classes. The entire day she was forced to just sit and do nothing because she couldn't see well enough to read or write. In art, she tried to draw a still-life sketch, though it turned out to be just a bunch of messy pencil marks in random places. She remembered her vision becoming blurry before just due to her progressively worse eyesight, but she still hadn't had this dramatic of a change in eyesight in such a short period of time.

Vidya's train of thought was interrupted when she heard somebody calling her name. "Vidya Reddy," the optometrist called, mispronouncing her name with a Southern accent.

"I'll just wait here while they do their check-up," Anu said as Vidya walked toward the optometrist.

The optometrist then silently led her through a dimly lit corridor and into a bright spacious room. Posters of eyewear covered nearly every inch of wall space and various instruments used for testing eyesight were scattered about the room. Blinking because of the intense fluorescent light that hurt her eyes, Vidya shifted her large glasses onto the bridge of her nose.

"Please take a seat," the optometrist said in a cold steely voice. Obeying instructions, Vidya sat upon the cushiony pink stool in the back of the room. "Now, you are telling me that your vision was fine yesterday, but suddenly today everything is extremely blurry," the optometrist asked skeptically.

"Yes. I can't read or write because everything is so hazy," Vidya responded.

Scribbling a few notes on a sheet of paper, the optometrist asked, "May I examine your glasses for a moment?" Vidya removed her glasses and handed them over to the optometrist. "No smudges, or scratches, they're crystal clear." Vidya heard the optometrist quietly muttering to herself. Handing the large glasses back to Vidya, the optometrist scrawled a couple more notes on the piece of paper. "All right, remove your glasses. Now we are going to test your eyesight to see if it has gotten any worse," the optometrist ordered. Vidya set down her glasses as the optometrist walked over to the far side of the room and stood next to a poster with several lines of characters that got progressively smaller each row down.

"Now cover your right eye with your hand and tell me what you see," the optometrist said, pointing at the line with the largest characters.

"E, 3, M, W . . ." Vidya recited as the optometrist pointed to the large letters and numbers. Gradually Vidya worked her way down to the third line. *I've never gotten through the first two lines before without messing up at least once.* Vidya could tell that the optometrist noticed that Vidya was performing better from the puzzled look on the optometrist's face. Now Vidya was down to the fourth line without a single mistake. *It seems as if things look less blurry without my glasses,* she thought as she continued blurting out the characters. Finally, she was down to the sixth line and each miniscule letter and number looked as clear as day from twenty feet away. With each successive correctly recited letter or number, the optometrist's face became redder and redder with surprise.

As soon as Vidya finished the entire chart without a mistake, the optometrist furiously scribbled more notes on the sheet of paper. "Now, let's do the same for the other eye."

Again, Vidya completed the entire chart without a single mistake. Crumpling up the piece of paper with the messy notes and throwing it in the trash, the optometrist walked toward Vidya. "Well, how do I put this?" the optometrist said. "For some unknown reason, you're eyesight has become miraculously sharper overnight. You went from 20/100 vision, extremely bad eyesight, to over 20/10, which is much better than average. The reason that you were seeing blurry today is because your glasses were actually impairing your vision, not aiding it. I don't know how it happened, but you don't need your glasses anymore."

Strangely, Vidya wasn't as happy as she thought she would be. The prospect of not needing to wear her glasses was joyful, though she was filled with the curiosity of how such a miraculous change could occur. *How did my eyes suddenly change from needing extremely powerful lenses to having vision that is sharper than the average person?*

Veer could already smell the unmistakable aroma of Indian spinach pakora wafting down from the top floor of the four-story apartment complex as soon as he stepped inside of the building. Easily holding his hefty backpack in his left arm, Veer headed toward the stairs. He was surprised to see his brother leap up the stairs three at a time with speed he never thought a thirteen-year-old could possess. What shocked him even more was the fact that Jai hadn't stopped to pant and struggle for breath at the first landing, and continued on. As he scratched his itchy rash, Veer followed, a ways behind.

As Veer hustled up the stairs, he remembered the spark of happiness he saw in his brother's eye, something that Veer thought had vanished since their father's disappearance. When Veer asked him how he did in physical fitness testing, his brother refused to answer and said he would tell Veer when they reached home. Though when they reached the familiar bus stop at the corner of Acorn and Beacon Streets, instead of heading toward their large house down the sidewalk, they crossed the street and walked into a small apartment complex. This building was where Vidya and Anu's apartment was located. Vidya's apartment was the brothers' home away from home ever since early childhood. Since both families' houses were so close, since Veer could remember, everyone visited both houses on a daily basis, and treated each as home.

Veer's thoughts were interrupted as Jai knocked loudly on the wooden door. Veer heard the clanking and clattering of metal pans as Anu bustled toward the front door of the apartment. Veer and Jai were greeted with a warm welcome as Anu ushered them inside. Instantly feeling comfortable as soon as he stepped in the small but cozy apartment, Veer saw Vidya doing her homework at the kitchen counter while snacking on the tempting pakora. Anu immediately handed both of the brothers plates topped high with the delectable crunchy vegetable fritters and continued to fry more of the tasty treats.

As Veer and Jai approached the kitchen counter, they instantaneously noticed something different about her; something was missing.

"Glasses!" Veer blurted out as soon as he realized what Vidya was missing, startling everyone in the room. "Where are your glasses?"

"Vidya has some important news to tell you!" Anu said in an excited voice.

"You'll never believe this," Vidya paused, adding to the feeling of anticipation. "But you know how my vision was suddenly blurry this morning and I had to go to the optometrist?" she asked and Jai and Veer nodded. "Well, that was because my eyes had miraculously gotten better, and my glasses were hindering my eyesight. The optometrist said that my vision changed from 20/100 vision at my last visit a month ago, to under 20/10, which is better than normal, possibly overnight. So basically, I don't need my glasses anymore." With each word, Veer and Jai's mouths opened wider and wider with both excitement and surprise. "I know it is strange but it's perfectly true, because I can see you guys clearer than I ever could before." Vidya ended her dramatic announcement with a vigorous rubbing of the rash around her eyes.

Jai was speechless in shock and seemed to be contemplating something, though Veer had a much different reaction and was bombarding Vidya with questions. "How is that possible? So you never need to wear glasses again? Not even contacts? How did they test your eyesight?" Veer interrogated his friend. As Vidya started to answer all of these rapid-fire questions, Veer noticed that Jai wasn't even paying attention and guessed that his mind was meandering through other thoughts.

After Vidya answered all of Veer's many questions, Jai finally spoke. "Ever since yesterday, one strange event upon another keeps on occurring and I'm pretty sure this all can't just be coincidental. Well, something weird happened to me today too. To make a long story short, I improved my mile time by ten minutes and thirty-two seconds, and I even beat the Medley school record for the mile run. I basically just sprinted the entire mile and didn't even have to use my inhaler. It's as if I woke up this morning and my asthma just disappeared. Not only were my lungs cured of asthma, but also they became stronger than an average person's. Also, the muscles in my legs felt ten times stronger, and I can run faster than ever before," Jai said in a matter-of-fact voice. Once Veer heard Jai's news, his head started to spin out of both excitement and shock in knowing that he too had a drastic improvement in an area he used lack in.

"Are you okay, Veer?" Vidya asked with a concerned look on her face when she saw Veer's woozy expression.

Shaking his head and expelling the dizzy sensation, Veer scratched the itchy rash on his arm and spoke. "Yeah, I'm fine. It's just that the weirdest thing happened to me today too," he began. "Once I touched the pull-up bar, expecting Mr. Randolph to give me two weeks of detention for a bad score, something really strange occurred. My body felt almost weightless as my arms pulled me above the bar, and I just kept repeating the motion until I became tired. I ultimately had to stop at thirty-two pull-ups, but I also beat the Medley School Record. I don't know how I did it, but I'm pretty sure that improving from zero pull-ups to thirty-two isn't just a coincidence or a fluke," Veer finished.

"How is it possible that all three of us immensely improved in the areas that we used to be especially weak in?" Vidya posed the question that was in all of their minds. The question seemed to hang in the air as a long silence followed, and no one was able to find an answer.

"Well, why don't you guys mull it over while snacking on a new batch of sizzling hot pakora?" Anu said breaking the silence, as she scooped the fritters out of the bubbling oil in the wok and heaped it onto the three plates. Their mousi always gave practical and helpful advice for almost everything, ranging from homework to chores, and they could constantly rely on her to help with tough decisions and difficult questions. "You three are smart; just put your heads together and I'm sure you'll be able to figure something out."

As Veer munched on the delectable pakora, he looked down at his scrawny arms, not able to believe what had happened to him, Jai, and Vidya today. As his mind drifted, he remembered all of the strange events that had occurred over the past few days: First the sighting of the mysterious trench coat figure, then the weird rash, and now this. *Could all of these events be connected?*

CHAPTER 5

Veer rapidly rang the doorbell as he waited on the porch alongside Jai and Vidya. After finishing up the scrumptious new batch of pakora while contemplating the recent strange happenings, the trio headed toward Veer and Jai's house. Soon the grand double doors swung open, and Jyothi quietly ushered them inside.

Muttering something about finishing up some work, Jyothi headed upstairs, though she seemed preoccupied by other thoughts. Ever since Samir's disappearance, Jyothi always seemed distracted and lost. The trio waited until her frail figure was no longer in sight.

"I still can't believe what happened today," Vidya said excitedly. "All three of us mysteriously gaining new strengths; it just seems like stuff out of a comic book."

"Yeah, I know. I just can't wait until the Medley of Talents contest now. We're surely going to win the arm wrestling event with my newfound strength and the race with Jai's speed," Veer said as he easily threw his backpack on the table as if it were a football.

"I'm just glad I don't need glasses anymore," Vidya said cheerfully looking around the kitchen as if she had never seen it before.

"That's all great, but we still don't know how all of this happened," Jai stated as he scratched the rash on his leg. "And until we do, it'd be best if we all don't go blabbing to everyone about our new strengths," he continued and the other two agreed.

"I just hope that these strengths are not just temporary, though," Veer said.

"Yeah, I really don't want to ever have to put on those huge annoying glasses again," Vidya added. *Brrring!* The loud ringing of the phone interrupted the trio's conversation. "I got it," Jai called as he sprinted to the phone with amazing speed. After muttering a few words into the mouthpiece, he shouted, "Vidya, it's for you, Mousi is calling." He handed the phone to Vidya. As she grasped the silver telephone, it slipped out of her hands and plummeted to the floor. *Crrack!* The telephone hit the floor with devastating impact, splitting the phone in two and creating a loud noise.

"Oops, I'm so sorry," Vidya squeaked as she bent down to pick up the two halves of the phone. As she examined the remnant pieces of the phone, something caught her eye. When she looked closer, she saw a thin wire protruding from the mouthpiece of the phone. "Hey, guys, is this supposed to be in your phone?"

"I don't see anything," Jai responded irritably.

"Here, look," Vidya said tugging on the wire and suddenly a small bright green object resembling a computer chip emerged.

"Looks like it was inserted in there . . .," Jai responded, taken aback.

"Strange," Veer added, looking shocked. "And I don't think it's supposed to be in there, and only Vidya could see the wire, I couldn't see it at all."

"I guess it's my newfound microscopic vision," Vidya said. Then suddenly Jai, without warning, ripped the chip out of the phone and snapped it in half.

"What are you doing?" Veer said, stunned by Jai's actions. Vidya was too shocked to ask any questions.

"Well, when I saw that chip, it looked familiar. Then I saw the logo on the chip and remembered where I had seen it before, when Nanna and I read about cool electronic devices at the Spy Museum in DC. I read that those specific chips were extremely high-tech and were going to be used for gathering highly classified information. You know, reconnaissance. I'm guessing that they can use the hardware already built into the phones in order to listen to what we are saying. But the thing is, these chips aren't supposed to be out on the market for another year or two. Even the CIA hasn't supposed to have gotten their hands on them. Somebody is trying to listen in on our conversations, and track what we are doing at every single moment. Whoever they are, they must really want to know what's happening in this household." Jai finished in a quiet voice as the others listened intently.

After a couple of silent, tense moments, Veer finally spoke. "Who are they, and why do they want to know what we're doing?" he wondered.

"Do you think it's got anything to do with the mysterious figure at school and at this house?" Vidya asked.

"I don't know, but it'd be best if we kept all of these conversations away from this house, because I'm not sure how many more bugs they've got disguised around here," Jai stated. "But just try to act as normal as possible, as if all of this just never happened. If they find out that we figured out that they are tracking us, who knows what could happen," he said whispering to the others.

"Well, since we can't have all of these discussions here, then we should agree on somewhere else to hold them," Vidya whispered.

"Yeah, Vidya's right," Veer agreed. "I think we should meet at school or at Vidya's house."

"I'll check for bugs around my apartment just to be sure," Vidya responded. "We have no idea how far these people have gone. It's better to be safe than sorry." The other two nodded in agreement.

On the afternoon of the next day, Veer sat in front of Mr. Harrison waiting for Jai and Vidya to show up. As their new Medley of Talents coach, Mr. Harrison scheduled their first team meeting after school to start practicing for the competition.

As Veer sat waiting, several thoughts flooded into his mind. *Why in the world would someone want to stalk our every move? How long have these "bugs" been planted in our house? Who put them there?* Veer was filled with mixed feelings of fear, anxiety, and excitement after their recent discovery of the bug in their phone.

As minutes passed by, Veer's mind shifted to other thoughts. The school day had been fairly uneventful. Students either patted him on the back for his recent accomplishment of breaking the pull-up record, or just gaped in astonishment. For the first time this school year, the band of bullies didn't try to bother him in fear that they would be the ones getting beaten up instead. Veer enjoyed all of the compliments and not being constantly annoyed by the troop of bullies as a result of his recent accomplishment, but Jai just had to spoil all of the fun by telling him he couldn't utter a single word about his pull-up score. *Jai can be such a party pooper sometimes,* he thought angrily.

Veer's thoughts were interrupted when a loud knock sounded at the door and Mr. Harrison replied with a gruff "Come in." Opening the door to the principal's office, Jai slipped inside quietly and took a seat next to Veer facing Mr. Harrison. After a few more minutes, Vidya finally entered the principal's office as well.

"All right then, now that you are all here we can begin our first team meeting during which we will start preparing for the Medley of Talents competition. We've got three months until the competition, so I want you to use your time wisely," he began. "So first things first, have you guys decided which person is going to compete in each competition?" he asked.

"Yeah, we've decided. I think I'm going to do the music and arm wrestling events, Vidya's going to do the writing event, and Jai's going to do the math event and the race," Veer replied

"Okay, got it," Mr. Harrison grunted back as he scribbled on his notepad. "Now the next thing on the agenda is for me to give you a couple of things to help you guys practice for your events," he said as he pulled something out from under his desk. Grunting and turning red with effort, Mr. Harrison hefted a heavy box onto the table. Veer could barely see writing that was hidden under a thick layer of dust that had accumulated on top of the box. Swiping the coat of dust with his right hand, Veer could now see familiar impeccable handwriting scratched in permanent marker. It read:

MEDLEY OF TALENTS
SAMIR GUPTA

As soon as he saw the name printed on top of the box with Samir's unmistakable neat handwriting, Veer was shocked, and from the looks on Jai and Vidya's faces, they were surprised as well. "Why is my dad's name on that box in his own handwriting? Did it used to belong to him?"

"Now that's just the thing," Mr. Harrison started off. "Before your dad went missing, he left a couple of things with me. He said he wanted me to give these to you to help you guys practice for the Medley of Talents competition, that's why I asked to be your coach. He also told me not to tell anyone but his two kids and Vidya. I don't know why he asked me to do that, but that's all I know."

"Why would he want to give us things to practice with a year in advance?" Jai asked.

"I'm telling you, I have no idea. I asked your father the very same question a year ago, and he told me that it would be easier if I didn't know," the principal responded. "I am very curious about the contents of this box ever since. Now if you want to see what's in the box as much as I do, let's get moving," he said as he hastily cut off the duct tape on the box and opened up its flaps. Removing the first item that he handed to Veer, he said, "Here's a brand new guitar tuner for the musician." Veer solemnly accepted the tuner, remembering when Samir had first given him a guitar for his tenth birthday.

"And a fountain pen for the author." Mr. Harrison passed the beautiful pen over to Vidya.

"The most advanced scientific graphing calculator for the mathematician." The principal handed the large calculator to Jai who took it with a curious expression. "As well as a stopwatch for the runner." Mr. Harrison handed this to Jai as well.

"And the last and certainly the heaviest, the dumbbell weights for the arm-wrestler." Mr. Harrison struggled to heave the two large weights into Veer's hands. He looked surprised when Veer handled the weights with ease.

"One more important thing," Mr. Harrison added. "Your father said to never speak about the contents of this box with anybody else. I know it sounds strange, but I am only telling you what he told me." The trio was puzzled, but agreed to follow Samir's instructions.

The rest of the meeting passed by quickly as the others discussed practice schedules and contest strategies, though Veer's mind was wandering through other thoughts. *Why did Nanna give these items to Mr. Harrison? And like Jai said, why did Nanna give them to the principal a year in advance of the competition?* Finally, their coach ended the team meeting with an announcement.

"All right, guys, study and train hard, follow the schedule we came up with, and try to use those items Samir left you to help you practice. Remember, teachers aren't going to pile on the homework for the next few months due to the upcoming competition, so utilize this opportunity to practice as much as possible." Mr. Harrison convened the team meeting.

Glimpses of various familiar stores flew past Veer's eyes as he stared out of the car window, his mind wandering. After the meeting with Principal Harrison, he, Jai, and Vidya waited for Anu to pick them up. While they were waiting, and even after they got in Anu's car, Vidya was chattering excitedly about her practice schedule in anticipation of the Medley of Talents competition coming up in a couple of months. Though all the while, Veer was distractedly staring off into the distance as he was unable to take his mind of his nanna ever since he saw Samir's name printed on the box that Mr. Harrison gave them.

Fond memories of his father washed over Veer like a pleasant wave of happiness. Ever since Veer could remember, his nanna was always spending every spare moment with his family. Though he was a hard-working doctor, Samir had always found time to play with Veer and his brother and teach them interesting things. Besides his job as a plastic surgeon, Samir had a hobby that he greatly enjoyed: working with all sorts of technology from computers to cell phones. Since Samir's early childhood, as Veer could recall his nanna explaining to him, Samir loved playing with technological gadgets and was what people would call a "tech genius." As Samir gained more and more knowledge about the wide range of technology, he liked to pass this information on to his children, teaching them about all of the cool gadgets he'd encountered. This is why he would always take Jai and Veer to various technology museums in and around DC. Veer and Jai both greatly enjoyed these visits as well as all of their time spent with their father. Samir was overall just an amazing person to be around, and Veer just wished he could have more time to spend having fun with him.

The only weakness that Veer could recall about Samir was his hardness of hearing. Since he was nearly deaf, Samir needed powerful hearing aids ever since he was little. Though many others thought that this condition was a serious problem, Samir just thought of his hearing troubles as yet another challenge to conquer. This characteristic of Samir was what truly surprised Veer; Samir's constant enthusiasm was never dampened by problems, but actually fueled by them, for he thought of every problem as a challenge to find a solution to.

Samir had truly been involved in every aspect of Veer and Jai's lives. From school to sports, their father had always been there to cheer them on. Samir had been very supportive of their studies, constantly helping them with homework. Also, for the year before he went missing, Samir had been extremely active in their school, planning the new Medley of Talents competition. Throughout that year, their father had several meetings with Mr. Harrison, discussing the events, guidelines, and prizes. Not only had their father been involved in school, but in extracurricular activities as well. Though Veer and Jai hadn't been skilled in sports, Samir insisted on them participating in some sort of athletic activity. Since both Veer and Jai had decided to play basketball, Samir chose to be their team coach. Veer and Jai appreciated their father's determination and fairness to the entire team.

As Veer's mind continued to wander, he couldn't help but think about the curious box with his father's name printed on it. *Why in the world would he give a box filled with miscellaneous items to practice for the competition a year in advance of Medley of Talents?* Veer racked his brain for an answer to this question, but he came up with nothing after several minutes.

Veer stared out the window as Anu's car pulled up the long driveway leading to his house. Shuddering as he remembered the recent narrow escape from the mysterious person near the house, Veer unbuckled his seatbelt when the car finally slowed to a stop. *Hopefully that's the last of those guys,* Veer thought as he woke up Jai, who had fallen asleep on the ride home from school.

When Veer pushed the car door, it flew open, almost breaking off the chassis. "Sorry, I guess I'm not used to my strength yet."

As Veer made his way to the front door alongside Jai and Vidya, he thought he heard fallen leaves crunching underfoot. Glancing over to the front yard on his right, Veer was sure he spotted something. Looking closer, Veer saw a dark hunched-over figure darting from tree to tree. *I guess it isn't the last of them,* Veer thought grimly as he caught up to Jai and Vidya.

CHAPTER 6

Vidya twirled her beautiful fountain pen between her fingers as she stared blankly through the window of her apartment. Scanning the scene outside, noticing every detail with her keen eyesight, Vidya began to observe the first signs of winter: leafless trees, barren landscape, and the occasional scurrying of animals preparing for hibernation. Letting out a big sigh, Vidya glanced down at the blank lined sheet of paper in front of her.

It had been like this every single day of the four weeks since the meeting with her Medley of Talents coach Mr. Harrison. At the beginning, she had been so excited about preparing for the competition, and she promised herself that she would practice every single day. But each and every time she sat down to write, she just couldn't think of a topic to write about. She would always end up jotting down some mediocre essay or poem that just wouldn't cut it for the Medley competition. She needed a spectacular unique piece of writing that would impress the judges.

Today she had taken out the fountain pen that Samir had given her, thinking it may somehow help her find a better topic to write about. *So far it isn't helping one bit,* she thought to herself as she examined the elegant mahogany colored pen. As she continued to appreciate the amazing handiwork that went into making the pretty fountain pen, a thought popped into her mind. *That's it! I could write about Uncle for the competition.* As she considered the idea, joyous memories of Samir enveloped her.

As soon as Veer and Jai's father met Vidya, he had treated her like she was part of his own family. Samir would constantly dote on her like he would have his own daughter, showering her with gifts and toys. Since Vidya's father passed away when she was a small child, she had always thought of Samir as a father figure. And therefore when Samir disappeared, she was just as devastated as Veer and Jai. *I still can't believe that he just vanished.*

After Vidya recollected her memories of Samir, she finally became focused once more on the task at hand, practicing for Medley of Talents. Then she gathered up her thoughts and made a mental outline for her essay. *Just one more thing: the title. Hmm, maybe "Samir Gupta's Influence on Me." Naa, too boring. How about "Samir Gupta: Family Member, Friend, and Role Model." Yeah, that sounds good.* Once Vidya decided upon a fitting title for her essay, she began to print it on the top of the lined paper in her usual neat handwriting. But once the pen touched the paper, no ink flowed out. Shaking the pen vigorously, Vidya tried twice more but to no avail. *I guess the pen doesn't have any ink.* Vidya unscrewed the top of the pen in order to confirm that the pen was inkless. As she did so, an idea struck her, *Wait, but why would Uncle give me a pen that doesn't work?* Shrugging, Vidya pulled off the top of the fountain pen. She then shook the pen in order to remove any possible ink cartridge, but instead of a cartridge falling out, a small scrap of paper fluttered to the floor. *What in the world?* Vidya thought as she bent down to pick up the piece of paper off the linoleum floor. It read:

BABBLE LATEST TALK

Scratching her head in puzzlement, Vidya wondered what the clue was referring to. She closed her eyes and repeated the phrase over and over again. *What is Uncle trying to tell me? This phrase doesn't mean anything!* She thought of each of the words individually and tried to find some connection that the words had with Samir. But she came up with nothing.

Vidya's mind drifted to other thoughts as she stared at the raindrops hitting her window. She reminisced about the time she spent with Samir. He had this special ability to make everything fun. Whenever she, Veer, and Jai were stuck at home and bored on rainy weekend days like today, Samir always found something exciting to do. He often gave them interesting brainteasers to solve. Vidya remembered sitting with Veer and Jai at the kitchen table, frantically trying to solve the brainteaser first while Samir gave them small hints. Every time the brainteaser involved any type of math, Veer or Jai would always seem to get it first. But Vidya was the queen of word puzzles; she was especially good at unscrambling anagrams. Every time Samir gave them a set of scrambled letters, Veer and Jai would give up, and Vidya would solve the anagram in a matter of seconds.

Vidya felt herself getting off track. Glancing up at the clock, she realized she had spent over an hour reminiscing. *I just can't focus. I'd better take a break and try a little later.* With that resolution in mind, she bundled up in her thick coat and went to Veer and Jai's house to see what her friends were up to.

Vidya repeatedly pressed the doorbell at Veer and Jai's house, shivering in the chilly breeze of late autumn as the gentle pitter-patter sound of light rain traveled to her ears. Though she was supposed to be taking a break from the clue, she still couldn't get it out of her mind. *Why would Uncle leave a slip of paper with a senseless phrase in my fountain pen?*

Finally the door swung open to reveal a dismal expression on Veer's face. "Oh, hey, Vidya." Veer greeted her in a bored tone. "Come in." Vidya followed him inside the house.

Veer led her to the spacious living room where Jai was fiddling around with a paper clip with a bleak expression similar to Veer's. "Hi, Vidya," he mumbled, not looking up from the paper clip in his fingers.

"Hey, Jai," Vidya said cheerfully. "Why is everyone so gloomy?"

"We're bored," Both Veer and Jai responded at the same time.

"Why?"

"Well, it's raining outside so there's nothing to do, Amma's at work, none of our friends are home except you. And you were practicing for Medley of Talents," Veer responded.

"Yeah, and why couldn't *you* practice for Medley of Talents?" Vidya retorted hotly.

"Because it's raining outside and there is no space to run inside," Jai responded.

"How about you, Veer?"

"Well the weights that Nanna gave me are too light for me. It's so boring to keep on lifting them. I need a challenge."

"Then if you guys are so bored, then why don't you find something to do indoors, like a video game?" Vidya shrugged.

"I guess we could," Jai said reluctantly.

"How about that multiplayer basketball game that we always used to play? We haven't played that in a while. What was it called again?" Vidya wondered.

"Basketball Battle," Veer answered. As soon as Veer mentioned the video game, the three friends were swept over with grief. Basketball Battle was a game that they would always play with Samir, and all three of them could still remember the smile on his face whenever he played Basketball Battle with them. Because this specific video game reminded them of Samir, the three friends hadn't played Basketball Battle in over a year since he disappeared.

Shaking his head, Jai finally spoke, "We can't run away from this game forever just because it makes us think about Nanna. He would have wanted us to continue playing the game . . ."

But before Jai could utter another word, something clicked and Vidya interrupted him blurting out, "Wait that's it! Babble Latest Talk is an anagram for Basketball Battle!"

"What in the world?"

"It has to do with Uncle! But, remember, the bugs!" Vidya reminded them. "Let's just find the game then we'll bring it over to my house, where it's safe to talk. I'll explain everything later. I don't want to take any chances."

Jai could have easily sped ahead to find the video game before Veer and Vidya made it to the bottom of the stairs, but he decided to wait, not wanting to show off his powers in case someone was still watching through hidden bugs throughout the house.

The trio was too excited to speak as they raced to the box filled with the numerous video games that Veer and Jai owned, As she dashed through the basement, questions filled Vidya's mind. *What kind of secret message will Basketball Battle reveal? What does it have to do with Uncle?*

In excitement, Veer tried to pick up the box containing all of the video games in order to find Basketball Battle, but as soon as he laid a hand on it, the thick wooden box cracked in half under his strength. "Oops, I still can't control my strength yet," Veer whispered and shook his head in disappointment. Jai stifled a giggle.

"Focus! Let's find the game." Vidya sifted through the pile of video game cases. "Here it is!" she exclaimed as she held up a dusty video game case with Basketball Battle printed in large blue letters. The trio stuffed the video game case and the game system into Veer's school backpack and headed out the front door.

Once they reached Vidya's apartment, she told them about the mysterious slip of paper that had fallen out of the fountain pen that Samir had given her. She opened the video game case and examined the object with her keen eyesight, not missing a single minute detail. Then she popped out the disc to inspect it as well. After taking a few moments to contemplate the situation, she finally nodded her head when she reached a conclusion. "It doesn't look as if there are any concealed compartments where he could have hidden a slip of paper or any other small object. As I predicted, we probably have to play the game in order to find out whatever Uncle is trying to tell us."

The three friends eagerly unpacked the video game console, a sleek black and neon blue box, and plugged it in to Vidya's TV. They inserted the Basketball Battle game disc and crossed their fingers, hoping that the meaning of the clue would become clear.

"Do you think Uncle programmed a message to appear on the screen?" Vidya wondered excitedly.

"Maybe, I don't know," Veer muttered back as the game finally loaded and Basketball Battle appeared on the screen in large print. Grabbing one of the controllers, Jai quickly pressed start and selected the multiplayer option. The TV immediately changed to the select characters screen.

When the characters screen appeared on the TV, the three cursors that represent all three players immediately moved to a box at the top right of the screen on their own, without Veer, Jai, or Vidya touching their controllers that would normally control the cursors. This box contained a picture of the player named Julius Erving.

That's strange. Vidya wondered as she checked to make sure that her controller was on and functioning properly, and Veer and Jai did the same. The green lights on the back of the controller confirmed that their controllers were fine. *Hmm, if our controllers are working properly, then it must be the game that's causing this problem.*

When Vidya tried to move her cursor off Julius Erving and select her favorite player, Reggie Miller, the cursor just wouldn't move no matter how many times Vidya slammed the joystick on her controller in the opposite direction.

"It must be a glitch, let's reboot the console." Veer reached a conclusion.

Just as Veer was about to press the restart button on the video game console, Vidya blurted out, "Wait, Uncle reprogrammed the game so Erving is the only player we could play with. Let's just start the game and wait a little longer before rebooting the console."

The three of them simultaneously pressed the start button on their controllers and impatiently waited for the game to start, constantly fidgeting. They were playing a game of two-on-two basketball, but since there were only three of them, Jai decided to play on a team with a computer-controlled player. Finally after a long period of the game loading, the word start flashed across the screen in bright blue letters as a referee threw the ball into the air. Veer and Jai both jammed their joysticks up, trying to win the jump ball. Veer's player grabbed the ball first. He immediately tried to pass the ball to Vidya's player, but mistook her player for Jai's. Jai laughed mockingly at Veer as his player performed a 360-degree slam dunk.

"It's too confusing with all four players being Julius Erving!" Veer yelled in frustration.

The game was filled with turnovers, as each of them continued to get confused. Every other possession seemed to involve a pass to the opposite team, who would immediately dunk the ball into the basket. As the game wore on, each of them got more and more frustrated. By the end, Jai's team pulled ahead and barely won 11-10.

"Always number one!" Jai playfully shoved Veer.

"It's just because your team had a computer controlled player that didn't make as many mistakes as you did!" Veer retorted hotly.

"At least I didn't turn the ball over every single time I touched it!"

"Guys, it doesn't matter who won." Vidya found herself playing her usual role as mediator of the Gupta brothers. "We have to figure out what Uncle is trying to tell us."

The thought of their nanna quickly put a stop to their petty squabble. "I couldn't find anything else wacky with the game, other than that the only character we could play with was Erving," Jai said.

"Do you think he was trying to tell us something by only letting us play with Erving, or it was just another game glitch? The game is over five years old," Veer said.

"I don't know. Does Julius Erving have any connection to something that could help us find Uncle?"

"Julius Erving, also known by his nickname Dr. J, was a professional American basketball player from 1971-1987." Jai was already sitting at the computer, reading off the monitor.

"How did you get over there that fast?"

Jai simply stretched his legs and smiled. "He was known for his dominant dunking ability." Jai squinted his eyes and scrolled down the page. "Awards, blah, blah, blah, personal life, stats, career." He continued to skim. "Nothing here seems to be useful."

"Hmmm, maybe we missed something. Let's play the game again and pay closer attention," Vidya suggested.

Just as they were about to press the start button on their controllers, the phone rang.

"I got it." Jai sprinted toward the phone and was there in less than a second.

Has he gotten even faster? Vidya wondered.

"Veer, Amma just got home and wants us to come back. Vidya, she says you should come too if you are not too busy."

The trio ran through the rain back toward the Gupta household. Vidya walked into the kitchen to find Jyothi, who she always called Aunty. As Jai greeted his mother, Vidya noticed how his skinny body looked huge compared to his mom's petite and fragile frame. "How was everybody's day?"

"Fine," Veer responded. "Jai and I couldn't practice for the Medley Competition, it was too rainy outside, and I need heavy weights. We played Basketball Battle for a while and then went over to Vidya's house to play cards." He told a white lie.

Vidya knew why Veer wasn't telling his mother the full truth. He didn't want to include his mother in the search for Samir, knowing that if they were unsuccessful she would sink deeper into depression. Also, Samir had specifically told them not to discuss the contents of the box with anybody.

"That sounds fun," Jyothi said half-heartedly, and Vidya knew that she was thinking about Samir as soon as Veer uttered the name of their favorite videogame. "How does a dinner of hot roti and dal sound?" she said, changing the topic, as she rolled up her sleeves.

"Awesome, sounds yummy," Vidya said.

"All right, then I'd better get started making it."

As she was washing her hands, Jyothi chuckled. "I remember that Samir would only play video games with four people. He would play with you three, and he also loved to play whenever he met up with his old medical school friend, Dr. Juarez."

Vidya was startled when Jai grabbed her arm. "Dr. J!" he whispered.

"What?"

"That's what Nanna was trying to tell us by only allowing us to select Erving!"

Veers eyes widened with excitement. It took a second for Vidya to put it together. *Dr. J must refer to Dr. Juarez!*

"Can you tell us more about him?" Veer asked Jyothi.

"Sure," Jyothi replied as she began to gather her ingredients and the various instruments she would need to make the classic Indian combo of roti and dal.

"Samir knew Dr. Juarez ever since medical school. They had become friends as they were both studying to become plastic surgeons, having the common goal of helping restore happiness to those who suffered birth defects or horrible accidents," Jyothi explained as she set a steel bowl, rolling pin, and a pan on the counter. As she removed flour, salt, and vegetable oil from the cabinet below the stove, she continued, "You guys probably won't remember, but Dr. Juarez came over to our house when you guys were toddlers. Ever since, I heard about him through Samir. Your nanna always described him as a kind man and a doctor that truly cared for his patients."

Jyothi then poured the wheat flour into the steel bowl and sprinkled salt on top of it. She then drizzled vegetable oil on top. "The last time I saw him was two years ago, when I dropped Samir at the airport for that flight to India on the Save the Smile effort. The two of them were truly dedicated to that program, always willing to sacrifice time to help those desperately in need of plastic surgery who couldn't afford it. They went to many impoverished places together, such as the poor villages in India, providing free surgery to children born with genetic cosmetic defects like a cleft palate." Jyothi placed a measuring cup under the faucet and let a thin stream of warm water flow in. She then emptied the cup into the steel bowl and started mixing all of the ingredients. Jyothi stirred the flour using her hand; the dough got thicker by the second as it was combined with the water and oil. She repeated this process over and over as the small soft pillow of dough in the center of the bowl gradually grew larger. Finally she removed the dough and began kneading it against the marble counter.

"Also, the two of them took shifts at the same hospital and occasionally saw each other there. Both of them were known to be excellent surgeons and the rest of the doctors there respected them greatly," Jyothi said. After kneading the dough repeatedly, she removed a small ball of dough from the rest and pressed it against the marble counter. The dough formed a thick circular pancake. She used the rolling pin to compress it into a thin flat patty, about the thickness of piecrust. Next, she turned on the stove and placed a special type of grill used exclusively for making rotis on top of the flame. It was shaped like a minitable, having three metal legs and a flat circular surface on top with metal bars spanning from end to end of the circle. Jyothi set the roti on the grill and it immediately inflated into a hollow sphere, puffing up to the size of a softball. After waiting a couple of minutes and flipping it, Jyothi removed the roti and placed it on a plate. She then poked a hole in its thin exterior and it deflated even faster than it had inflated. As she repeated this process of heating the rotis, she continued, "Your nanna was extremely fond of Dr. Juarez's wit. He always said he cracked the most hilarious jokes."

"Just wait a second while your rotis cool and I'll heat up the dal that Mousi made earlier today." Jyothi removed a glass container filled with the delectable spiced lentils and set it in the microwave for thirty seconds.

"So if Uncle and Dr. Juarez were such good friends, how come we didn't get to meet him again?" Vidya inquired.

"Well, Samir never brought his work into his home life. He almost never talked about work with you guys and rarely even with me. When was the last time you remember that Nanna's colleagues came over to our house?"

"Never," Veer responded and the other two agreed. The microwave started beeping, and Jyothi removed the dal. She spooned it out alongside the rotis and handed the plates to Veer, Jai, and Vidya. Veer and Jai devoured their rotis, rapidly ripping off chunks and using them to scoop large mountains of dal.

"Thanks for telling us, Amma!" Veer said through mouthfuls of the savory roti.

Before Vidya even began to take a single bite of her first roti, the boys were already calling for seconds. Vidya gently tore of a piece of the roti by using her thumb, forefinger, and middle finger, the traditional Indian method of eating roti. She then folded this piece and scooped up the dal, taking a bite. There was an explosion of flavors in her mouth, and she could taste the dozens of spices used to make the delicious meal.

Once Vidya finished her first roti, Veer and Jai were already patting there stomachs, each having eaten five. "Come on, Vidya, hurry up!" Veer called. Vidya gradually finished her meal, enjoying every single bite, savoring not only the many flavors but the contrasting textures of the creamy dal with the thin, light, chewy roti. After three rotis, she complimented the chef. "Thanks Aunty, those were some of the best roti I've had in a while."

"You're not going to eat more?" Jyothi asked. "You never eat enough."

"What are you talking about? I'm stuffed," she said patting her stomach. Jyothi just shook her head laughing. "Do you need help cleaning up, Aunty?

"No, no, I got it covered. Besides, Veer and Jai are calling you."

Vidya headed into the family room, where Veer and Jai were lounging on sofas.

"Finally! You always take forever to eat," Veer muttered. "Do you think that Nanna was trying to tell us about Dr. Juarez through the game?" he whispered.

"I think so. We couldn't find anything else wrong with the game, except that our characters were locked on Dr. Juarez. So what do we do from here?"

"Well we shouldn't discuss this anymore at home," Jai said. "I know it seems paranoid to keep on heading over to Vidya's place whenever we discuss the clues, but we have to assume that someone is always listening in."

"Jai's right," Vidya replied. "Besides, you guys have to pick up your game console anyway."

With that, the three of them told Jyothi where they were going and set off to Vidya's house. As soon as their mansion was out of view, Jai excitedly raced ahead in the fading sunlight, reaching Vidya's apartment before Vidya and Veer made it to the street corner. The two of them finally reached Vidya's apartment building, greeted by Jai.

The trio then climbed the many stairs up to Vidya's apartment. Once they swung open the door to the cozy apartment, they were immediately welcomed by Anu.

"Hey, guys."

"Hi, Ma, when did you get back?"

"Just a couple of minutes ago, my doctor's appointment was prolonged because the office was behind schedule. What did you guys have for dinner?"

"Roti and dal," Veer responded.

"Sounds good. I'm just going to whip up some dinner for myself right now. Do you guys want anything?"

"We just had dinner, Ma."

"I know, but you guys never eat enough."

The trio then headed into Vidya's room, which was tucked away in the back corner of the comfy apartment.

"So what do you propose we do now?" Jai asked.

"Well, if Nanna wanted us to know about Dr. Juarez, we should probably look him up on the Internet." Veer came up with a solution.

"Good idea!" Vidya exclaimed. "Let's use the computer in Ma's room."

The three of them headed across the hall into Anu's room and sat near the computer in the corner. Vidya pushed the power button. After a minute or two, the desktop was loaded onto the screen. Vidya clicked on the Internet icon, and after another couple of seconds, the computer loaded to its homepage. Vidya typed in the URL of the widely used search engine called Nonillion, her fingers flying over the keyboard. Once Nonillion showed up on the screen, Vidya entered "Dr. Juarez" in the search bar and hit the enter key. After waiting a couple of more seconds, dozens of results popped up on screen. Vidya clicked on the first one, labeled "Plastic Surgeons of Northern Virginia." Once the web paged popped up, Vidya scrolled down with Veer and Jai watching intently.

Vidya was the first to spot the words "Dr. Juarez" with her keen eyes. It read: Dr. Juarez is the head of the practice of Plastic Surgeons of Northern Virginia. He graduated from Johns Hopkins medical school with an MD as well a PhD in biotechnology. He currently has an office in Vienna, Virginia.

"Does it say anything else about him?" Jai wondered. Vidya scrolled down further to the end of the page, but couldn't find anything else. She also clicked some of the next couple of links listed on Nonillion, but not much more information could be found.

"All right, so it doesn't tell much about him on the Internet. How else can we find out more about him?" Veer wondered.

"We could meet him," Vidya proposed.

"That's true. It's the only way we could find out more," Jai said logically.

"But how are we going to do that?" Veer asked. "His office is too far away to walk to, and it will sound strange if we asked Amma or Mousi to drive us there."

"Why don't we ask Amma if we could invite him over?" Jai said.

"No, I don't think it's a good idea. With the bugs around our house, we have no idea who is listening," Veer responded.

"That's right," Vidya said. After a couple of moments of silence, Vidya suddenly exclaimed, "I've got it! Judging by the address listed here, his office isn't too far away from the Vienna Mall. It won't sound strange if we ask someone to drop us off there. Then, from the mall, we could walk to his office, talk to him, and come back and ask someone to pick us up."

"That could work," Jai said.

"When are we going to do this?" Veer asked. "We've got to do it while Dr. Juarez is at work, so it has to be on a weekday.

"How about this Friday, after school? That's when most kids go to the mall anyway, so it will be even less suspicious. We could pretend to go to a movie, and then walk over to his office," Vidya responded.

"But there still is one more problem. How are we going to convince him to talk to us at work?" Jai asked.

"I'd bet he'd make time in between appointments to see his best friend's kids."

"That's true," Jai said.

Their conversation was interrupted when Anu opened the door. "Hey, guys, sorry to interrupt, but Jyothi just called and said that Veer and Jai have got to get to bed soon because they have basketball tryouts early in the morning tomorrow."

"Okay, we're coming, Mousi," Jai responded.

After she closed the door, Vidya said, "All right, then it's decided. On Friday, we'll go talk to him and find out what Uncle was trying to tell us."

With that agreement in mind, the trio disbanded, all excited about the recent discovery and looking forward to the meeting with Dr. Juarez.

"So, how do you think you did on the math test, Veer?" Vidya asked.

"It was pretty easy, but the extra credit was hard. Did you get eighty over eighty-one for the extra credit?"

"Yeah, I think so," she answered.

The three of them were in Anu's car on the way to Vienna Mall, supposedly to see the newest hit movie *Polymorphous*, about alien shape-shifters invading earth. But really they were bristling with excitement, anticipating their meeting with Dr. Juarez.

After a short ride, Anu's ancient faded red station wagon swerved into the large parking lot of Vienna Mall. Screeching to a halt in front of the movie theater entrance, the trio exited the car and pretended to head toward the movie theater.

"Are you sure that you don't want me to come inside the theater with you?" Anu asked, filled with motherly anxiety. "You won't even know that I'm there."

"No, Ma, we'll be fine," said Vidya.

"Okay, but if you need me, just call and I'll be here in a second. Bye!"

The three of them waved goodbye and walked toward the mall entrance, just in case Anu was still watching. Once they saw the red station wagon pull out of the parking lot, they started talking excitedly in hushed voices.

"All right, I looked up the location of Dr. Juarez's office. We have to head left on Autumn Boulevard then left again on Deciduous Street. His address is 1989 Deciduous Street. Just follow me," Vidya told the other two and they nodded in agreement.

The trio walked briskly toward the outskirts of the mall, headed for Autumn Boulevard, which bordered the mall on the left side. Huddling together in the chilly late autumn breeze, they shared their predictions of what would happen in the meeting with Dr. Juarez.

"Do you think he will help us find Nanna?" Veer wondered hopefully.

"I don't know, but obviously Nanna wanted us to find him. He left us with the anagram that was decrypted into Basketball Battle, and when we played the game, it led us straight to Dr. Juarez," Jai replied. "What I still don't get is why Nanna left the anagram in the pen inside the Medley of Talents box and gave it to Mr. Harrison?"

"Yeah, I was wondering the same thing," Vidya said.

The three walked in silence down Autumn Boulevard until they reached Deciduous Street. Following Vidya's directions, they crossed the street and headed down the sidewalk veering away from Vienna Mall. They walked a while longer until they reached a small cluster of office buildings after seeing nothing but residential neighborhoods.

"Here it is," Vidya said once the trio walked past the parking lot and toward a five-story gray building. They entered into a small lobby and headed straight into an elevator. "I think it's on the fifth floor," she told Veer and Jai, then confirmed by checking the slip of paper containing the address of the office, and stowed it back in her coat pocket.

Jai hit the dented old button indicating floor five on the elevator panel, which then lit up with a bright orange light. The old elevator steadily rose, and cheesy elevator music emanated from the speaker in the upper left hand corner. Finally the elevator stopped, and the metal doors slid open to reveal a narrow hallway.

"It's number 535," Vidya said. They stopped at the second door on the right. "Are you sure we should do this?" she wondered apprehensively as she set her hand on the doorknob.

"Yeah, come on let's go," Jai replied confidently.

The trio entered a spacious waiting room with chairs lining the edges. A few patients sat reading magazines or newspapers. The three of them walked nervously up to the secretary sitting behind a counter on the right side of the room.

"When is your appointment?" the secretary asked gruffly, not even bothering to look up from her desk. Once she did look up, she raised an eyebrow in surprise, not expecting three kids alone in a plastic surgeon's office.

"Umm, actually we're not here for an appointment," Veer started off.

"Yeah, we were wondering if we could briefly talk to Dr. Juarez. We're his friend's kids," Jai continued.

"Dr. Juarez is extremely busy. I'm sorry, but he won't have time to see you today," she said very matter-of-factly.

"Please, it will only take a couple of minutes," Vidya begged, though the secretary kept a stern face and simply shook her head.

"Fine, then we'll just have to wait here. We can wait all we want," Jai responded coolly.

"All right, the office closes at 9:00 PM. That means you guys have got to wait, let me see," the secretary said in an uncaring tone, checking her watch. "Four hours."

The trio sat side by side in the comfortable armchairs at the opposite end of the waiting room. Vidya anxiously glanced at the clock, then the secretary, then back at the clock again, wondering whether the secretary was really going to make them wait that long. Finally, after thirty nerve-wracking minutes, the secretary spoke.

"You guys are seriously willing to wait that long to see Dr. Juarez?" the secretary said. "You're persistent, maybe crazy, but still persistent," she said, picking up the phone and rapidly dialing a number. "Dr. Juarez, hi this is Linda. Three kids are waiting in the front to have a conversation with you. They said they are your friend's kids. I told them that you were busy, but they just won't leave. I guess you'll have to talk to them."

The trio silently celebrated with high-fives all around, for all of that time waiting paid off. After a few more minutes, a tall lanky man strode into the waiting room clad in a white coat. He had a long face, thick mustache, and striking blue eyes.

"Hi, Linda, are those the kids you were talking about?" he said in a barely noticeable Spanish accent, pointing to Veer, Jai, and Vidya. The secretary nodded. He paced over to where the three of them were sitting. "Do you know that thanks to you, I had to stop midway in a surgery and the patient's face was mutilated?" Dr. Juarez reprimanded them sternly.

What? Vidya was shocked. She looked around at Veer and Jai who bore similarly surprised faces. Then the secretary's raucous guffawing broke the tension, and Dr. Juarez's stern face cracked into a wide grin.

"Don't you guys know how to have any fun?" he said bumping playfully into Veer. Vidya remembered Jyothi saying something about Dr. Juarez's hilarious wit, but the last joke didn't seem too funny when she saw her friends' stunned expressions.

After taking a moment to collect himself from the recent shock, Jai introduced himself as well as Veer and Vidya. "Hi I'm Jai Gupta and this is my brother Veer Gupta. We're . . ."

"Samir's sons." Dr. Juarez finished Jai's sentence. Immediately his wide grin disappeared and his normally buoyant demeanor turned into sadness.

"And this is our friend Vidya Reddy," Jai continued. "We were wondering if we could talk to you about our father."

"Sure," Dr. Juarez immediately responded. "First, let's find somewhere more private to talk. Could you guys follow me to my office in the back?"

"Are you sure that we're not interrupting? I mean the secretary said you had a lot of patients waiting," Veer wondered.

"No, it's fine. I would do anything for Samir's kids. My colleague can cover for me for a while," Dr. Juarez said as he ushered the trio into his office.

Vidya entered a small office. The walls were decorated with awards and plaques. Three chairs lay scattered about the room and another was behind a wide desk. Dr. Juarez gestured for them to sit down as he closed the door and took his own seat.

After everyone had taken their seats, Dr. Juarez asked, "So what do you want to know about Samir?"

"Well, we want to know anything about our dad aside from his home life, which we already know about, and more about him as a plastic surgeon, which you know about," Veer started off. "See, we were playing this game . . ." Veer paused, wondering if he should tell Dr. Juarez about the anagram. Veer glanced over to Jai, who shook his head warning him not to, and Vidya could understand why. Besides, they haven't even told their families about it yet, so they shouldn't go rushing to tell strangers about the anagram. "Never mind," Veer continued.

"Well, I knew your father since medical school, as you probably know . . .," Dr. Juarez started off. He went on to share many anecdotes of his experiences with Samir at the renowned Erudite School of Medicine. Though Dr. Juarez told them many interesting stories about their years in training, Vidya couldn't glean any useful information. She did not hear anything especially important that Samir would want them to know or a reason that Samir would want them to talk to Dr. Juarez.

Vidya's ears perked up when she heard Dr. Juarez change the topic of conversation from medical school to the trip that he and Samir had taken two years ago on the Save the Smile effort. *Maybe this is why Uncle wanted us to see Dr. Juarez, to learn more about the trip that they had taken.* He described how both of them were huge supporters of Save the Smile, a program in which plastic surgeons traveled all over the world to impoverished places to provide free surgeries to rectify particular congenital defects for those who couldn't afford to pay. On this trip,

Dr. Juarez and Samir went to many places in India where the people were living in penury. Dr. Juarez also told them how he and Samir had together performed over seventy pediatric plastic surgeries.

He also told them that at one point during the trip, they had split up. He traveled to Hyderabad, a large city, while Samir had visited Patnam, a small village in South India. Then Dr. Juarez continued to explain their trip when they joined back together. He told them everything from what food they ate to the surgical instruments they used. The longer Dr. Juarez talked and talked, the more and more Vidya was discouraged that they would gain any helpful information from their discussion. Finally after an hour of hearing Dr. Juarez's voice, Vidya heard someone else speak again.

"So is there anything else that you would know about our father that we don't already know?" Veer asked.

"Well, we really bonded during medical school and the trip we took together. We used to meet more often a long time ago, when you guys were small. But we both got busy with work, and we would only occasionally see each other at the hospital. But there is nothing much to say about those brief meetings. We would simply greet each other, maybe share a few things about our family members. He was especially fond of talking about you guys." Dr. Juarez had a warm smile. "Time was limited in between seeing patients, so we wouldn't have much time to talk," Dr. Juarez responded.

"Well, I guess we've gotten what we came for," Jai said. "Thank you, Dr. Juarez," he continued, getting up to shake Dr. Juarez's hand firmly. Veer did the same, and Vidya could hardly suppress a laugh when she saw Dr.

Juarez's face turn beet red with pain after Veer's crushing handshake. Vidya also shook his hand and bade goodbye.

"I'd better get back to seeing my patients," Dr. Juarez told them. "If you need anything else, just call my cell phone. Let me know if I can help your family in any way," He said as he opened the door. With that, the trio left Dr. Juarez's office and headed down the elevator. As they descended, Vidya couldn't help expressing her utter disappointment after the meeting.

"No real important information came from that meeting," Vidya sighed.

"Yeah, nothing that would help us find Nanna," Veer said, depressed.

"What was Nanna trying to tell us?" Jai pondered also showing signs of frustration.

The trio then exited the office building and walked back to Vienna Mall where they would be picked up by Anu. *Maybe we're going down the wrong track,* Vidya thought.

CHAPTER 7

J ai anxiously shifted his legs from side to side as he
waited in the uncomfortable chairs in the doctor's
office alongside Veer, Vidya, Anu, and Jyothi. They
were here because of the chronic itchy rash that had now
spread to the palms of their hands and soles of their feet.
It had bothered them ever since the beginning of school,
starting with that unpleasant visit to the nurse's office, and
the rash never went away. Immediately, once they got home
that day, Jyothi had called the pediatrician, but the office
was so backed up that they couldn't get an appointment
until December 14. So here they were now, hoping that the
doctor could make something of this bizarre rash.

As time passed, Jai's thoughts floated elsewhere. He
couldn't help but think about the disappointing meeting
with Dr. Juarez the week before. Jai had actually thought
they were on to something with the anagram and
Basketball Battle. Maybe his nanna was trying to tell them
something, something that would help them find him.
But the meeting with Dr. Juarez yielded no important
information that would help them. *Man, I shouldn't have
gotten my hopes up,* Jai thought.

"Jai Gupta, the doctor is ready to see you," the nurse
finally called after a lengthy waiting period. Jyothi and

Jai walked together down the bright fluorescent bulb-lit corridor lined with exam rooms on each side. At the end of the corridor, they stopped in front of a large exam room. "You can take a seat, and the doctor will be with you shortly," she said briskly, and then immediately shut the door. Jai could smell the scent of alcohol, bleach, and sterilizing chemicals that characterized a doctor's office. Jyothi sat down on the wooden chair at the edge of the room, while Jai propped himself up on the soft bench covered with a sheet of thin disposable paper.

As they waited for the doctor, Jai glanced around the room in boredom. Lining the walls were posters showing various parts of the human body. Another poster described preventive measures to protect you from germs. The floor was covered with blank white tiles, and combined with the glaring white walls, gave the room a very sterile feel.

After a couple more minutes of waiting, the doorknob turned and the door swung open to reveal a cheery looking pediatrician. "Hey, my name is Dr. Brown!" he said buoyantly as he flipped through the three charts. "So, Jai, you came here because of a chronic rash. Can you describe the symptoms to me?"

"It is extremely itchy, and spread throughout our entire body," Jai replied.

"It could be an allergic reaction. When did the symptoms first appear?"

"About three months ago," Jyothi said.

"Normally allergic reactions don't last that long. It's probably viral. Hmmm, I guess we'll have to run some tests to diagnose this," Dr. Brown pondered aloud. "Sorry, we'll have to draw blood. Don't worry, I promise it won't hurt too much, and at the end you can have one of these super-cool Band-Aids," he said as he shook a transparent container filled with smiley-face Band-Aids. *I am not a baby anymore.* Jai rolled his eyes as the pediatrician prepared the syringe. Jai thought back to the times when a doctor mentioned a shot and he shriveled up in fear. He also remembered when he started to cry even before the doctor administered a shot, but afterward, he was content as long as he got a "cool" Band-Aid and a lollipop. He shuddered just thinking about it.

"All right, it will just be a small prick," the doctor reiterated as he positioned Jai's arm. Jai knew the doctor was just trying to quell any fear he may have had about getting blood drawn. *But come on, I am a teenager, I can handle it.* First, the doctor wrapped a tourniquet around Jai's upper forearm in order to expose the vein that ran through his arm. Then he slowly inserted the needle and began steadily drawing a small sample of blood. Then he carefully removed the tourniquet and needle and quickly put a smiley-face Band-Aid where the syringe had once been. *Why can't I just have a normal Band-Aid?* Jai thought as he pictured his friends laughing at the bandage on his arm.

"I am going to send this sample straight over to the lab. The tests will take a day or two. I am curious to see the results, because I have never seen anything quite like this before. Are you sure nothing else out of the ordinary happened to you, any other symptoms?" the doctor asked, wondering about this peculiar enigmatic rash.

He immediately shook his head vigorously and responded with a resounding no. The strange occurrences that had happened recently had to be kept confidential. Not even his family members knew about the sudden emergence of powers recently. He couldn't risk telling anyone, knowing that someone was constantly watching him.

After all three of them had been seen, they checked out in the waiting room. As Jyothi and Anu talked to the cheery secretary at the front desk, Jai once again thought about the meeting with Dr. Juarez. He just still couldn't accept that his nanna was gone, and until recently, he thought that maybe Dr. Juarez could help them locate him. Yet now, all hope seemed lost.

It was a surprisingly pleasant and warm day for the middle of January. With the Medley of Talents competition approaching in just a couple months, Jai and Veer had decided to train for the physical challenges in their huge backyard. Jai had just received word that for the running competition, there would be two races, a 100-meter dash, and a mile run. Today he was going to focus on endurance again, so he pulled out the stopwatch that he found in the box that Samir had given them. Yesterday, knowing that he was going to be out training today, Jai had figured out that exactly ten laps around their backyard was a mile. But he also remembered that long distance runners often trained at much higher distances than they would run in the race so that when the actual race came, it seemed like a piece of cake. So today, he decided on an even two miles.

As soon as he set foot on the grass, he clicked the start button on the stopwatch and immediately started at a breakneck pace. He took long even strides and short calculated breaths. Again he had the strange sensation that he was flying, almost as if his legs were numb. It took little effort to cover great lengths in miniscule amounts of time. It felt as if he was going even faster than when he had run the mile at school. And the best part about it was that he wasn't getting tired one bit; actually he was increasing his pace as time wore on.

Jai glanced at his brother who was training in the middle of the yard and couldn't help but snicker. Veer looked ridiculous as he was doing a one-handed handstand. Today, Veer mentioned something about testing the endurance of his muscles, not just their sheer strength. In order to do so, he was practicing handstands for long periods of time. It seemed logical, but as an older brother, Jai just thought it looked funny.

All right, halfway done, Jai thought after he completed ten laps. He kept on steadily increasing his pace and increasing his stride length. At the fifteenth lap, he was at a full sprint. It was after two more laps of all-out sprinting that the exhaustion started to seep in. *C'mon, Jai, you can do it.* He tried to encourage himself as sweat poured out. He started to feel a painful burning sensation in his legs, and remembering seventh grade biology class, immediately knew it was lactic acid building up due to his muscle cells not receiving oxygen in time. It took all the strength left in him to finish those last couple of laps, and he had to push himself to the limit. Finally when he reached the finish line, he hit the stop button on his stopwatch and collapsed in the soft dew-covered grass gasping for breath. Though he was tired, he felt good, knowing that he beat his previous record by a considerable amount. After waiting a couple more seconds to let the pain slowly relinquish from his legs, Jai got up to cool down and just see how fast his new time was.

Once Jai glanced at his stopwatch, he immediately knew something was wrong. All that the LED screen displayed was a jumble of letters and symbols that couldn't have corresponded to the time for his two-mile time.

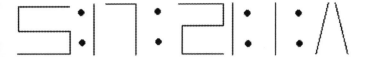

Five, seventeen, twenty-one, one, forward slash, back slash: what's that supposed to mean? Jai fiddled with the many buttons that covered the top of the stopwatch, yet the screen remained the same. *Idiot,* Jai thought to himself. *I was in such a rush to train, that I forgot to check to see if the stopwatch even worked.* Jai kept on trying to fix it, but to no avail. Now he would never know his time. "What is this good for?" Jai muttered to himself angrily as he threw the stopwatch into the grass.

"What's wrong?" Veer asked, still perched on one hand.

"The stupid stopwatch that Nanna gave us doesn't even work."

"Let me see it." Jai picked up the stopwatch from the grass, hung it around his neck, and walked over to Veer. As he was walking over, Veer suddenly yelped and toppled over into the grass. Again, Jai couldn't help but laugh.

"Stop it, Jai," Veer said as he got up and brushed the grass off his athletic clothes. "Now do you want to know why I fell over or not?"

"I know why. It's just because your muscles gave in." Jai was still snickering.

"No, actually it has nothing to do with that." Veer shot his brother a nasty look. "Turn the stopwatch upside down."

"Why?"

"Just do it."

"Fine." Jai sighed and rolled his eyes. When he turned the watch over and looked back down he couldn't manage to say anything but a surprised "wow."

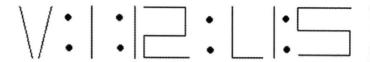

Virus is what the watch read.

"That's why I toppled over," Veer responded. Then suddenly, the thought came to Veer. "Do you think this is Nanna trying to tell us something again? I mean, this is the second time . . ."

"I don't know but we can't talk about it here!" Jai said in an alarmed whisper. "Let's go to Vidya's house."

With that, the two brothers raced up the block, Jai's feelings of exhaustion and anger wiped away by a sea of excitement. Once they were well away from their house and far from any unwelcomed visitor's view, Jai wasn't able to contain his excitement any longer and he sprinted at almost an inhuman speed to Vidya's apartment building.

"Veer, hurry up!" Jai impatiently waited for his brother at the apartment entrance. Finally, Veer arrived panting heavily in his effort to keep up with his brother. Together, they bounded up the stairs until they reached Vidya's floor. Jai knocked on the wooden door and the two brothers bounced excitedly, eagerly waiting to tell Vidya their finding. At last, the door swung open to reveal Vidya's face, which brightened upon seeing Jai and Veer.

"Hey, guys." Vidya greeted them.

"Hi, Vidya," Jai and Veer said together as they walked into the warm cozy apartment.

"Where is your mom?" Jai asked, trying to act normal and waiting for the right moment to reveal their discovery.

"In the shower. How did your training for Medley of Talents go?"

"It was good," Veer said. Unable to contain himself any longer, he blurted, "Vidya, we think we've found another clue!"

"What?" Vidya said, shocked. "But I thought it was over after the meeting with Dr. Juarez, I mean even you guys said it for yourselves."

"We thought so too, until a few minutes ago at least." Jai joined the conversation. "I had to admit that I was pretty skeptical too until Veer discovered it just now."

"Then what are you waiting for? Show it to me."

Jai pulled the stopwatch out of the pocket of his windbreaker. "This look familiar?"

"Yeah, it came from the box that Uncle gave to us. The same place I got my pen," Vidya said as she took the stopwatch from Jai to get a closer look. "Five, seventeen, twenty-one, one, forward slash, backslash; this doesn't mean anything, except that it's broken."

"Yeah, but turn it upside down," Veer told her.

"Wow." After that, Vidya was speechless for a few moments. Then she simply muttered "Virus." Handing back the stopwatch to Jai, she asked "How did you figure that out Veer?"

"Well, after Jai was finished running his laps and figured out that the stopwatch was broken, I asked to look at it. When he came over to me I was doing a handstand, which meant that I was seeing everything upside down. It was simply a mistake really."

"Who cares? All that matters is that we found another clue, and we know it's not a fluke now," Jai remarked.

"So what do you think it means?" Veer asked.

"Virus, virus, virus," Vidya repeated, pondering aloud. "It could mean a computer virus."

"It's an idea," Veer said.

"Sure let's go with that. But how is that supposed to mean anything? How will this help us find Nanna?" Jai responded, bursting the balloon of excitement. A long pensive silence followed.

"Well so far, we know two things, Dr. Juarez and computer virus." Veer broke the silence.

"Great, Sherlock Holmes. Tell me something I don't know," Jai said sarcastically.

Just as Veer was about to respond with a hot retort, Vidya said, "Well if we can't think of anything else, why don't we search the web? It can't hurt."

The trio hurried into Vidya's tucked-away room and crowded around the ancient desktop computer. Vidya clicked the Internet icon and it loaded the Nonillion web page.

"All right so should we input Dr. Juarez and computer virus?"

"Sure," the brothers responded.

Vidya quickly typed in the two keywords and pressed the search button. Three pictures of Dr. Juarez popped up, as well as a bunch of hot links. None of the results showed promising signs, all irrelevant to computer viruses.

"Figures," Jai said. "If Nanna wanted us to find something out, but tried so hard to put the information in clues so no one else would discover it, it probably wouldn't be on the Internet."

"That's true, but at least we tried," Vidya said, trying to improve the mood.

Jai's mind floated as he stared blankly at the screen. The picture of Dr. Juarez in his white coat reminded him of their recent visit to the doctor's office. All the tests had come back, and they said that their strange rash was due to some strange new virus, that hadn't been seen before.

But somehow the doctors had determined that it wasn't a serious illness and the rash would clear up soon. The idea hit him.

"Wait, that's it guys!"

"What?"

"I can't believe we hadn't thought of it already."

"What, Jai?" Veer and Vidya repeated. "Tell us already."

"What if the virus that Nanna is telling us about is a biological virus?"

"That does give a link between the two clues, they both relate to the medical profession," Veer pointed out.

"Exactly," Jai exclaimed.

"But we don't know enough now. I mean virus could mean any virus. That doesn't really help us with finding Nanna," Veer said.

"Uncle must have wanted us to know more," Vidya said. "We can't possibly determine anything from Dr. Juarez and virus, the two could mean anything."

"All I can say is keep your eyes peeled for more clues." Jai convened the meeting.

It was a foggy, chilly January day. It was the kind of day where you wouldn't want to be outside, especially at 6:30 A.M. But of course, being middle school students, Jai, Veer, and Vidya huddled, shivering, as they waited for their bus. Nevertheless, the trio was excited, still basking in the warmth of finding hope in the stopwatch clue.

Finally, the ancient yellow bus rolled up the hill, five minutes late. The trio quickly piled in the bus, hoping for warmth, but it didn't act as much of a shield against the brutal cold, as the heating system was almost always broken. This in combination with Jed, Gavin, and Sid snickering constantly made the long bus ride to school very unpleasant.

The day started off with Jai's least favorite subject, English. Most of the class period, while other students were reading poetry aloud, Jai stared into space, thinking of the stopwatch clue. *What other clues are there in store?* He wondered, his curiosity eating away at him. This was soon followed by a wave of fear. *What if Vidya was wrong, what happens if these are the only two clues? We have no idea what the two clues mean. Together they could represent thousands of things. What if we fail Nanna? What if we can't find him?* The utter despair of the idea deeply frightened Jai.

"Jai, Jai," his English teacher's voice broke his trance. "Read line 20-25 of the poem."

"Huh, oh sorry." Jai quickly flipped through his hefty textbook.

"You are usually on top of things; I can't believe you are acting this way." His English teacher eyed him sternly.

"Sorry," he repeated, then started to read the poem in a loud confident voice. Once finished, he tried to pay more attention until the rest of the period, but to no avail, as he started to drift off. Gladly, it was the sound of the ringing school bell rather than the voice of an angry teacher or worried friend that woke him up. He quickly collected his huge stack of books and rushed out into the sea of students that filled up the hallway.

Jai found his friend, Randy, waiting for him by the stairs. Jai first met Randy when they worked on a project together in shop class in seventh grade. Jed was also in their shop class, and initially he constantly picked on both Jai and Randy. The two of them decided to stick together against Jed, who then backed off.

"Hey, Jai, what's up?"

"Nothin' much. Anything interesting happen to you?"

"Na, but did you hear?"

"What?"

"That seventh grade kid, Sid, he beat your brother's pull-up record first period today. He did thirty-six man, that's four more than your brother."

"Seriously?"

"No joke man. That kid's strong."

As they continued to walk to second period together, Jai couldn't help but think about Medley of Talents. Ever since they discovered their powers, Jai thought they would breeze through the competition. Yet now, Sid broke the record his brother's record by a decent margin. Jai was beginning to wonder if they really did have a shot at winning this thing.

Up ahead, near Randy and Jai's second period classroom, a big commotion had started. Jai and his friend pushed through the excited crowd to see what was going on. In the center was Sid, in a black leather jacket that was patted constantly by admiring eighth graders. Beside him, were Jed and Gavin, for some reason taking in all the glory as well. Jed spotted Jai amongst the onlookers and shoved forcefully through the crowd.

"Hey Gupta!" Jed horribly mispronounced Jai's last name. "Our man Sid crushed your brother's record, and now you got no chance of winning the competition. So say goodbye to the golden trophy!"

"We'll have to see about that, Jed," Jai said confidently, but inside he was no longer sure that his team could win the Medley of Talents.

A whirlpool of thoughts swirled in Veer's head as he lay in his bed staring up at the ceiling. Earlier that day, Sid had handily beaten his pull-up record. When he saw Sid sneering at him on the bus and flexing his biceps, Veer's first reaction was anger. But even worse were the sinking feelings of disappointment and anxiety. *If I lose in the strength competition, we may end up losing the entire Medley of Talents.*

Veer looked over at his digital alarm clock, which read "2:34 AM." He moaned, knowing that he would have to get up to go to school in four short hours. He hated the nights when his body simply refused to fall asleep. He usually ended up checking his alarm clock every few minutes, though the minutes felt like hours. Veer would eventually fall asleep, but he would wake up feeling terrible the next morning and would feel tired and grumpy the whole day.

He flipped over his pillow and pressed his face against the soft cool fabric. He tried to rid himself of his anxious thoughts by thinking about the clues that they had found. *Dr. Juarez and Virus.* He repeated the words over and over in his head, but found no answers.

Suddenly a loud ringing noise interrupted his thoughts. *The alarm! Did someone break in?* Veer bolted upright and switched on the lights. Thinking quickly, he ran to his closet and started looking for something to defend himself with. After rummaging through the messy pile of miscellaneous items, he found his peewee baseball bat. *This will have to do. Besides, with my increased strength, hopefully I can stand up to the intruder.*

Veer quietly exited his room and tiptoed into the hallway. *If this guy has a gun, then the only chance I have is taking him by surprise.* When he was halfway down the hallway, Veer heard yelling. He immediately began sprinting toward the noise. As he got closer, he realized that it was Jai.

"Over here!"

Veer sprinted down two flights of stairs to the basement. Jai was standing next a shattered window with a shocked expression.

"What's going on?" Veer asked.

"As soon as I heard the alarm, I sprinted around the whole house trying to find out where someone had broken in."

"You should have waited for me." Veer patted his peewee bat. "What you did was incredibly dangerous."

"I know, but it was my first reaction," Jai replied. He gulped, "And the strange thing is, I realized that this is no robbery."

"What?" Veer was puzzled.

"Nothing was stolen. But take a look at this." Jai pointed to the wooden box that Veer had smashed earlier when he was looking for Basketball Battle. The video game cases that were once neatly stacked in piles were now strewn across the floor.

Veer gasped. "You think the intruder was looking for Basketball Battle?"

Jai shrugged. "Maybe, but they couldn't have gotten it, because it's in my room. All I know is that people are still watching us somehow, and they saw us rummaging through the video game cases. This has to be related. We have got to be more careful."

Veer heard footsteps coming from the stairs.

"Boys, are you all right?" Jyothi was panting.

"We're fine, Amma," They replied in unison.

"I've already called the police."

As Veer heard the sirens nearing his house, he felt plagued by a deep anxiety. Just a few minutes ago he was worried about losing Medley of Talents, and now someone had broken into his house. This was the first time since Samir disappeared that Veer felt scared. He looked out of the broken window and into the night. *Why are they watching us and what do they want?*

CHAPTER 8

Veer looked down at his pristine electric guitar and then closed his eyes as he ran his hand down the smooth neck. Samir gave Veer the beautiful guitar as a birthday present three years ago. Playing the guitar had been one of Veer's favorite hobbies until his father disappeared. Ever since, he could not play without feeling a pang of sadness. But now, he had to put aside his feelings and focus on improving his guitar skills. With the recent news of Sid breaking the pull-up record, the team couldn't afford to lose the nonphysical challenges. Veer had to truly excel at playing guitar, which meant he needed constant practice.

He began by placing his fingers the position of a simple *G* chord and started to strum. As soon as his pick hit the strings, an utterly horrible noise rang out. The guitar was horribly out-of-tune, probably because Veer hadn't picked it up in over two months. Veer looked around the room for his electric tuner, but then remembered to his dismay that he had lost it a few weeks earlier. Then an idea popped into his mind. *Oh yeah, Nanna gave me a guitar tuner in the Medley of Talents box. I could use that one instead.* Veer raced upstairs into his room, where the box was safely hidden from any unwanted visitors, tucked underneath his bed. He looked around his room, just to make sure no one was watching, and then Veer pulled the box out and blew away the dust that had caked on top of the lid. He carefully removed the lid and grabbed a small black box with a rectangular screen, the guitar tuner. Just like the stopwatch, it was one of the best and most accurate devices of its kind on the market. It could detect the slightest changes of pitch and displayed those changes on the wide LED screen.

Veer then headed back downstairs and on the way bumped into his brother, who had his nose buried in a giant math textbook as he walked. "Hey, Jai, watch it."

Jai looked up, unaware of what just happened. "Oh, sorry. I've just been so occupied trying to learn all of this math for the Medley Math Competition. It's extremely complicated. How's your guitar practice going?"

"Well, I needed to tune the guitar before I started, so I picked up the electric tuner that Nanna gave me."

"Oh," Jai said, not even paying attention. Then he continued to walk up the stairs, muttering some complex formula.

At least he is practicing, instead of trying to bother me. Veer headed back into the living room, where his guitar was waiting for him on the stand. Veer picked up the guitar and clipped the tuner on the end of it. First, he plucked the topmost and thickest string with his pick. The tuner almost instantly displayed a large bold *G. Wow that's really out of tune, way too high. It is supposed to be an E.* Veer turned the knob that was connected to the E-string counterclockwise and continued to pluck the string. Yet no matter how much he loosened the string and lowered the pitch, the tuner displayed a *G. That's funny, let's try the next string.*

Veer plucked the next string and the letter *A* came up on the tuner. *Good, at least that string is in the right pitch.* But, when Veer plucked the next string, again the string was supposedly way out of tune. Instead of showing a *D*, the tuner showed an *F*. Veer tried to tighten the string, but the tuner continued to show *F*. He continued to tighten the string, until it was on the verge of breaking. The same happened with the next string, the G-string. Instead of *G*, the tuner displayed another *F*, and no matter how much he altered the tension of the string, the tuner didn't change the note value. *That's impossible. Those two strings were at different pitches in the beginning. There is no way they were both F.* Veer was almost sure now that it was the tuner, not his guitar, that was broken.

Just to make sure, Veer continued on to the next string. For the fourth time, the same thing happened. Instead of showing *B*, the correct pitch of the string, the guitar displayed *A*. Strangely, for the last string, the tuner didn't display anything at all, the screen was just blank. This proved for sure that the tuner malfunctioned.

Great, now I have a broken tuner, so I can't practice at all today. This will throw me way off schedule with the Medley of Talents competition coming up so soon. Veer was getting mad. Unable to control his frustration, Veer grabbed the tuner and was just about to crush it with his bare hands when he remembered something. *Wait! The stopwatch and fountain pen that Nanna gave us in that box appeared to be broken, but actually contained clues! Maybe this does too . . .*

After taking moments to try to figure out how this clue was hidden in the guitar tuner, Veer came up with an idea. He plucked the strings quickly in succession, and five letters showed up one after another on the screen. "Gaffa" it ultimately spelled out. Veer had no idea what it meant, but he was sure it was a clue. He was so excited, he couldn't help but yell, "I found a clue!"

Within a few seconds, Jai was upon him. "Idiot!" he whispered angrily. "They are always watching us! Remember the intruder?"

Veer's cheerful mood was suddenly deflated. "I understand. But don't you want to know what I found?"

"Yes, but not here." Jai was pensive for a few moments. "We'll have to also tell Vidya about it, but she just called a few minutes ago saying that she wouldn't be available to practice until tomorrow. She has some sort of writing seminar. We're going to have to meet at her house tomorrow afternoon, after school."

Sunlight poured through the windows of Vidya's apartment. As always, a delicious snack was on the way with a savory smell wafting from the kitchen. Anu busily hurried about, preparing their snack with fastidious care. The trio was sitting around the dining table, excitedly discussing Veer's discovery.

"So you're saying that you were just tuning your guitar when it happened?" Vidya asked.

"Yeah, I had lost my guitar tuner, so I pulled out the one that Nanna gave us in the Medley of Talents box. But when I plucked the guitar strings I found that it was broken, or I should say it didn't serve its function as a tuner. When I plucked the strings in succession, it read G, A, F, F, A.

"Gaffa, what's that supposed to mean?" Jai asked.

"Is it even a word?" Vidya wondered. She quickly ran to her room and pulled out a dictionary that was sitting in her desk. She set it down on the kitchen table with a resounding thud and leafed through thin pages. "Nope. It just skips right over it."

"Think it's an acronym? I mean, if it isn't a word, then each letter could represent another word," Veer pointed out.

"Maybe, but how do we have any chance of finding the meaning of that acronym?" Vidya posed the question.

"That's true, each letter could represent thousands of words."

At that moment, Anu came in with a huge bowl of murukulu, savory fried Indian snacks. They were piping hot, right from the fryer, and of course, tasty. She made the snack by mixing the dough, then piping it out into shapes and sticking them into boiling oil. The result was spicy, salty, crunchy, and yummy. For a few moments, the only sound that could be heard was crunching, as the three of them gobbled down the snacks.

Once all of them had their fill, with plenty of murukulu left to spare, they continued the discussion. "All I can say is that we should try to find more clues."

"But how are we sure there are more clues? What if this is it? How are we going to find anything out?" Jai once again reminded them of the prospect of failure.

"I'm not sure. All we can do is hope," Vidya said.

"Jai, set the table!" Jyothi's voice rang out from the kitchen.

"'Kay." Jai paused the TV show he was watching and went to the kitchen to help his mom.

"They are going to be here any minute," Jyothi said, busily transferring all of the food she made into decorative pots. Today, Jyothi's colleagues from Vaccine Corp. were coming over for dinner. Being a high-level scientific advisor in the pharmaceutical company, Jyothi had many colleagues that were very high up in the corporate ladder. She'd even said that the vice president of the huge international company was coming today himself. But for some reason, Veer and Jai never really liked their amma's colleagues. They just couldn't put their fingers on why. They could also sense that their amma didn't like her colleagues either, but whenever they asked about it, she simply shrugged the question off by saying "they are nicer when you get to know them."

"And also ask your brother to help too," Jyothi called.

"Veer," Jai yelled. "Get your butt off the couch and come help."

"Jai, don't talk to your brother that way," Jyothi said almost automatically as she continued to prepare the food.

The two brothers grudgingly got the silverware and fancy plates as well as the placemats. They then went into the formal dining room (which they rarely used) and set everything down on the dark mahogany table.

"Don't forget to get water," Jyothi called and the two brothers lazily grunted in dismay. They reluctantly filled the pitcher with water and poured it into six glasses for themselves and their three guests from Vaccine Corp. After the two of them finished setting the table, the doorbell rang.

Jai swung open the wide double doors to greet unfriendly faces. The first man who entered was extremely thin and bony, had a long skinny neck, and a large hooked nose, looking almost like a raven. The other man who accompanied him had an appearance that was almost the opposite. He was very stocky and chubby, and had small beady eyes hidden under circular spectacles. Once they entered, the men just simply nodded at Jai and gave him their jackets.

"Okay, I guess I'll just put these in the closet." But when Jai looked up, the men were already walking toward the dining room. *At least they could say something.* Jai just shook his head and took the jackets to the closet.

A few moments later the vice president arrived, and Jai thought he looked even less lively than the other two men. He was hunched over and almost completely bald with a wispy ring of white hair surrounding his head. When Jai looked at the man's grey eyes shielded by thick enormous glasses, for some reason shivers just ran down his spine. Unlike the other two guests, the vice president at least introduced himself.

"Hello. My name is Dr. Schwartz," he said in a gravelly cold-hearted voice.

"I'm Jai." The man simply nodded in response. "Can I take your jacket?" Dr. Schwartz then just shook his head and hobbled into the dining room. Jai followed him into the spacious dining room where the aroma of delicious homemade food filled the air.

Jyothi finally entered the room and sat alongside Veer. "Sorry about that, just tidying up a bit. These are my sons Veer and Jai," she said, breaking the silence. "And Veer and Jai, this is Mr. Black," she said pointing at the tall raven-like man. "And Mr. Baker," She said as she pointed at the chubby man. "And lastly, you've both heard about Dr. Schwartz." Each man nodded when introduced.

A short silence followed, then Jyothi once again was the only one to talk. "Why doesn't everyone start digging into the food? Today I made pesto pasta with some tomatoes, baby spinach, and broiled cheese on top. I hope you like it." And indeed it did look good. The soft tubes of penne where smothered in a pesto sauce. The baby spinach garnish as well as the tomatoes added texture to the excellent taste of the dish. It was an exquisite homemade meal.

After everybody had taken their share and eaten a few bites, the conversation shifted to work, Vaccine Corp. business.

"I'm proud to announce that profits have increased by five percent in just the past month. This excellent meal should be considered a celebration. Cheers all around," Dr. Schwartz said very unenthusiastically, almost as if the speech were memorized.

Veer and Jai both phased out and enjoyed their food while the rest talked about the boring politics in the company. Just as Jai was in the middle of shoveling in his fourth helping of the delicious pasta, Mr. Black said, "Excuse me, Jyothi, would you mind telling me where the bathroom is."

"Oh, of course, Jai, can you please show Mr. Black to the bathroom."

"Sure." Jai got up and led the tall man out of the dining room, past the kitchen, and into a small corridor with the bathroom. "Here it is."

Again Mr. Black simply nodded. Jai went back into the dining room and just as he was about to take another bite, he was interrupted once again. The electronic automated vacuum cleaner had automatically started to clean and was making a loud noise. "I'll go turn that off," Jai said even before Jyothi asked.

He walked over to the study next to the kitchen, where the vacuum cleaner started its cleaning routine. The circular robot cleaner was proceeding along the edge of the room, using motion sensors to determine the specific path. Fumbling through the drawer in the study, he finally found the remote to the cleaner and pressed the off button. Just as he was about to return to the dining room to finish his meal, he caught sight of something in the corner of his eye. He turned to see a dark figure lurking about the family room. From the height and lankiness of the figure, as well as the hooked nose, he could tell it was Mr. Black. Jai slowly edged closer to see what was going on. Mr. Black was staring at the corner of the room, close to the ceiling. Jai followed his line of sight to see what he was looking so intently at. Jai was shocked.

Mr. Black was staring at the smashed camera that the trio destroyed while they had searched the house for bugs. Vidya had scanned every corner of the house to find bugs, and then they had disposed of them. That camera was one of those bugs, and Jai was sure that somebody who didn't know of the placement of bugs wouldn't be able to spot them (except for Vidya, with her improved vision, of course). That meant only one thing: Mr. Black somehow knew where the bugs were, and probably why they were placed there.

CHAPTER 9

"Amma, can you take me to the gym today?" Veer asked.

"Sorry, honey. I've got to run some errands."

"Can Mousi take me?"

"I think she has some guests over. But you can practice at home."

He nodded disappointedly and went upstairs to his room. A couple of days ago, when he'd heard that Sid had broken the pull-up record, Veer started his intense weight training. Before then, he'd thought he'd had the Medley Strength competition in the bag, but now it was a whole different story. Since Jyothi refused to buy Veer weights above twenty-five pounds, thinking it was too dangerous for him, he resolved to go to the gym daily where he could lift much heavier weights and use the exercise machines. He desperately needed to train if he wanted to win the Medley competition and simply doing push-ups or pull-ups at home wouldn't suffice.

Oh yeah, how about those dumbbells that Nanna gave me? They had been sitting untouched in the corner of his room accumulating dust, but now they would finally be of use. He walked over to them and picked up the larger dumbbell, which read forty-nine pounds, and the other read thirty-seven pounds. *What an odd selection of weights for dumbbells.* Usually weights ranged in multiples of five, starting with five and going up.

Veer curled the weight he had in hand. It seemed extremely light for forty-nine pounds, but then again, he had been constantly in the gym after school for almost a week now, lifting much heavier weights. He seemed to be getting exponentially stronger every day. In the fitness magazines he had been reading to learn how to build muscle and get stronger, they said that lifting weights with higher repetition would build strong lean muscle. So Veer started his routine with twenty reps of bicep curls in sets of ten with the forty-nine-pound weight for each hand.

Veer kept good form by standing with his back straight and extending his arm fully. Sweat started to pour and his arms began to hurt after ten reps. He started to grunt with the last five, but he endured. He finally finished his right arm exercises. Taking a deep breath, Veer took a short rest, and then picked up the dumbbell with his left arm. Just as he was about to curl the weight, someone banged on his door.

"Yo, Veer, open up!" Jai called. Veer swung open the door to reveal his brother, who was dressed in athletic attire and cradling a basketball in his arm.

"Wanna shoot some hoops? Our first practice with our new team is tomorrow." Veer didn't hear what his brother was saying. All he could stare at was the number 49 emblazoned across his brother's old basketball jersey. His old jersey number was 37. Then it struck him. *49 and 37-those are the weights of the dumbbells.*

"Hello, Veer. Earth to Veer." Jai was waving a hand in front of his face. "Answer!"

But Veer was lost in thought. Finally, he responded, "Jai, I think it's another clue." He started to explain his discovery as he raced to his closet and hastily sorted through his clothes, looking for his own #37 jersey. After a bit of searching through his messy closet, Veer pulled out his maroon jersey. He finished expounding his discovery of the clue to Jai by saying "So I'm thinking that Nanna hid something somewhere on these jerseys."

The two brothers thoroughly searched the inside of the jerseys, but to no avail. They didn't find anything hidden within the folds of their old basketball uniforms.

"The tags!" Jai exclaimed. And sure enough, at the bottom of the tags, some strange symbols were stitched into the fabric.

Jai's tag read:

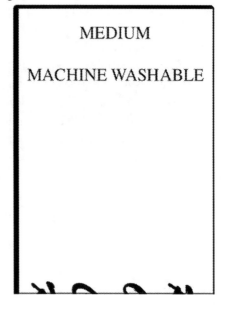

Veer's tag read:

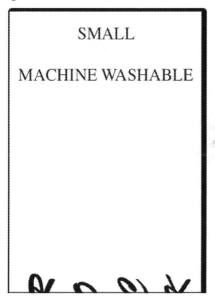

"What are they supposed to mean?" Veer asked.

"How would I know?" Jai responded.

The two brothers spent the next half hour trying to decode the symbols and deduce what Samir was trying to tell them.

"It's impossible, there's no way we're finding out anything," Veer said disappointedly after intensely contemplating the strange figures on the tags. "I give up."

"Would Nanna have wanted you to give up? Besides, let's think through this logically," Jai proposed. "If he stitched something on both tags, maybe we're supposed to use both of them to solve the clue."

Veer just sighed. "Fine, but I don't think we will get anywhere."

"Hand me your jersey." Jai stared at both tags. "Maybe one is a key for the other."

"Na. If we can't understand any of them, how are we supposed to use one to decipher the other?" he asked.

"Right. But how about if we try to place them next to each other? Maybe when combined, the symbols actually mean something." Jai was now trying to put the tags together in different configurations. "I've got it!" he finally said as he held the tags up to show Veer.

"Rock," Veer read aloud. "What's that supposed to mean?"

Jai was deep in thought. His brow was furrowed and he clenched his jaw. "The word rock could refer to anything. But the fact that it's printed on the tags of our basketball jerseys could help us."

The two brothers pondered for a couple of moments.

"Wait, didn't our old assistant basketball coach always tell us to 'pass the rock'?" Veer broke the silence.

"True, he did always refer to the ball as the rock. I guess he was pretty old school that way," Jai responded.

"Maybe Nanna was trying to lead us somewhere. The weights led to us finding the jerseys, so why wouldn't the jerseys lead us to something else, like a ball?'

"We could try it."

With that, the two boys raced downstairs and into their garage, where they kept all of the sporting equipment.

They rummaged through the box that contained soccer balls, baseball gloves, and footballs. They hadn't used their old ball in years because its grip had worn away from years of play. But now, they needed it more than ever. After reaching the bottom of the crate, they finally triumphantly pulled out the mud-encrusted old basketball.

Veer inspected it all around. "I don't see anything different about it."

"Look closer." Jai was pointing at the words below the logo, which used to say Official Size, but now several letters were scratched out

It now read:

F A IZE

"Faize." Veer repeated the word imprinted on the basketball over and over, letting the word roll around in his mouth. "It doesn't ring any bells for me."

"Me neither. But saying it a hundred times won't help us, especially if *they* are watching. It looks like we're going to have another team meeting. Maybe Vidya might have an idea." Jai methodically went about with dealing with the situation.

Since Vidya was at another writing seminar, preparing herself as much as possible before her Medley of Talents writing event, the brothers resolved to tell her about the word the next day at school.

It turned out that Vidya had no idea about the meaning of Faize either. But she proposed that they go to the school library at lunch to research it.

"We could try. But we've researched the other clues and we've never been successful at deciphering them," Jai said pessimistically. "Nanna wouldn't give us clues just so we could look them up on the Internet."

"But it could lead us somewhere that might give us more information." Vidya persisted.

"Come on, Jai. We have to try." Veer agreed with Vidya. "Besides, it will be hard for them to track us at a school library."

Jai finally agreed after a considerable amount of argument, and the trio resolved to meet at lunch just as the bell for first period rang.

After an uneventful first couple of periods, Veer met up with the others in the library at lunch. They huddled around one of the library's four thick outdated desktop computers and began to surf the web. After thirty minutes of visiting every search engine and scrolling through pages upon pages of text on topics from indoor lighting to pizzerias, they gave up. The trio could not find one relevant piece of information, nothing to help them find Samir, and they went to their next classes disappointed and hopeless.

The rhythmic bouncing of the basketball calmed Veer as he assessed the situation on court. As the shortest player on his team, by default he was point guard, putting a lot of pressure on him to call the right plays. But in practice scrimmage situations like these, the nerves didn't get to him. The opposing players had set up a two-three zone, and immediately he knew the perfect play to call against this type of defense, the classic pick-and-roll. He flashed a two with his fingers to signal the offense. *Here I go.* Jason, Veer's burly redhead teammate, stood right behind Veer's defender to block his path, which was the perfect pick. Veer flew by his defender, who had slammed into the pick while attempting to guard Veer. The defense quickly adjusted to the play, sending three men to prevent Veer from scoring. When he saw this, Veer smiled to himself. *They fell for the oldest trick in the book, pick-and-roll.*

Now Jason was completely open, with no one in his vicinity to stop from scoring with the basket directly in front of him. Veer pushed the ball to Jason, executing the textbook chest pass. But as soon as the ball left his hands, Veer realized it was going way too fast. When the ball met Jason's outstretched fingers, Veer heard a yelp and Jason collapsed to the floor in pain. Veer had lost control of his strength.

He rushed over to help Jason to his feet. Jason was caressing a huge swollen finger that was beginning to turn a nasty blue purple color from bruising.

"You okay? I'm extremely sorry, man," Veer said as he walked Jason over to the sideline.

"Yeah, I'll be fine after I ice it," Jason replied between clenched teeth. "But good play call, man. I hope it'll work in the game on Saturday."

"Me too. You better rest that finger so you can play in the game. No one else on the team can set that good of a pick. It was as if my defender ran into a brick wall," Veer said as he patted his injured teammate on the back.

Just as Veer was about to rejoin the scrimmage, he heard his name being called. "Hey, Veer, get over here!" Veer turned around to see his new team coach calling him and his blood turned cold. Coach Smith was notorious for his harshness on his players, but his tough coaching usually led to championship winning teams. Immediately pessimistic thoughts started flowing through Veer's head. *He's probably going to punish me somehow. He's going to make me run suicides, or sprints, or maybe even laps outside in the freezing cold. I hope I'll only have to do push-ups.*

Luckily it was none of the above. "Veer, I like the aggressive play out there. Just put a little less heat on the ball. You're a point guard, not a pitcher."

Veer nodded his head respectfully and replied, "All right, got it, Coach."

The rest of the scrimmage was an extremely close, fast-paced game, and Veer was careful to control his strength. After twenty more minutes of play, everybody on the team except for Jai was panting heavily and sweating profusely. Yet Coach Smith forced them to continue playing, threatening to make them run unless they played with twice the ferocity. Ten more grueling minutes passed by before Coach Smith finally gave them a water break.

As Veer waited in line for the water fountain, he was suddenly yanked aside by Jai.

"Hey! What's the big deal?

"What's the big deal? What's the big deal?" Jai mocked Veer in an angry whisper. "You just revealed your power in the public."

"I didn't mean to."

"It doesn't matter. We've already had a close call, and I will not let you risk our safety again. We've got to lie low, Veer."

Veer just walked away angrily. *Jai just doesn't want me to show off,* he thought immaturely. But after Veer had time to cool off his anger and take a long drink of water, he started to see Jai's point of view. Last time they were lucky, but if it happened again, they could be seriously hurt. Even though he never meant to show off his strength, any displays of their powers in public could endanger them. It was better to be safe than sorry.

After their quick water break, the team started to do some layup drills. Coach Smith was obsessed with getting the fundamentals of basketball down before anything else, and he believed it was the key to success. So they began to practice the simplest shot in basketball, the lay-up. The team lined up on both sides of the basket at the half court line. One line did lay-ups as the other got their rebounds and passed the ball to the next person in the lay-up line. It was a basic drill, but it improved the team's ability to score layups in pressure situations, when everything was on the line. The drill worked even better when Coach Smith threatened them with suicides if they missed a single lay-up.

When it was Jai's turn to do the drill, he caught the rebounder's pass and immediately accelerated astonishingly fast toward the basket. But Jai was going way too fast and before he knew it he was behind the backboard. Veer could not help but crack up laughing.

He was quickly quieted by Coach Smith. "What's so funny, Veer? Your brother has just earned you and the rest of the team ten minutes of sprinting drills. Isn't that just great?" coach yelled. "And you, Jai, what are you doing? This is not a track meet. Control the ball! It's not that hard."

Jai just shook his head in disappointment.

"Everyone on the baseline. NOW!"

The next ten minutes went by incredibly slowly, and each second was excruciatingly painful for Veer. With each trip across the court, Veer wanted to quit, but he pushed himself to the upper end of his limit. What annoyed Veer even more was that Jai, the one responsible for the team's punishment, was having no trouble whatsoever with the sprints. He casually strode back and forth across the gym floor, seeming as if he was jogging, yet he was easily beating second place by at least two floor lengths. Veer was thankful that the next team was waiting on the sideline to practice. If they hadn't been, Veer was sure Coach Smith would have made them run until midnight. The team waddled with sore legs, groaning with each step, to the parking lot where their parents were going to pick them up.

It was pitch dark outside with the only light coming from car headlights as one by one the team members were picked up until only Veer, Jai, and Coach Smith were left in the Medley Middle parking lot.

"Do you guys need a ride? I've got plenty of space in my sedan," Coach Smith offered.

"No thanks," Jai replied. "Our mom's usually late from work on Tuesdays."

"All right, see you guys at the game on Saturday. Remember that practice makes perfect." With that the coach sped away in his black BMW M6, the engine roaring.

After Coach Smith's departure, the parking lot was dead silent. After five more minutes of waiting Veer was beginning to wonder if his amma had forgotten about picking them up from practice. Ever since Samir disappeared over a year ago, Jyothi seemed so preoccupied that Veer would not put it past her to forget, even though he knew that his amma loved them more than anything. Just to make sure his amma was on her way, he asked his brother to call her.

"Hey, Jai, can you call Amma? It's getting a bit late." There was no response.

"Jai . . ."

Veer turned to see the horrific sight of Jai hanging in midair with a single colossal hand clamping down with a vice-like grip over his neck. A deep scar ran down the hand that belonged to a giant of a man completely shrouded by a black trench coat. Veer was so stunned that it took him a moment to react as the man swung Jai around as if he were a ragdoll. Just as the man was about to slam Jai headfirst into the ground, Veer snapped out of his trance. He balled his hand into a tight fist then coiled his bicep muscles. Veer threw his fist forward with all of his might in an enormous punch straight into the man's abdomen. The missile met its target and it was powerful enough to send the giant sprawling. When Veer went in to get a closer look of the assailant, he was surprised to find him gone. Veer could just make out the humongous figure sprinting away in the distance at a speed that he thought only Jai could achieve. *Who are these people and why do they want to hurt us?*

Veer ran over to help Jai up. Luckily Veer had acted soon enough, for Jai was conscious and in one piece. Nevertheless, Veer could see bruises that wrapped all the way around Jai's neck from when the man had nearly strangled him.

"Are you okay, Jai?"

"Thanks." This was all Jai could manage to sputter out, as he was still recovering from the stranglehold he had just experienced. After a few moments, he continued, "If it weren't for you Veer, I could have been knocked unconscious," he paused for a moment, "or worse."

"I've got your back, Jai. And I know you've got mine."

CHAPTER 10

I n front of Jai lay line upon line of complex geometric proofs that seemed indecipherable at the moment. His math teacher, Mr. Steel, was a challenging teacher to say the least. This was the very reason Jai asked him to help prepare for the Medley of Talents math competition that was scheduled to be held next week. Mr. Steel agreed and gave Jai a problem set to complete at home. After spending nearly an hour on the first problem and not achieving anything except for successfully shooting ten crumpled pieces of paper into the trash can on the other side of the room, Jai skipped down to the next problem. *Finally, I get a break.* It was a simple statistics problem. This problem was a piece of cake, he just needed to plug a few numbers into his calculator and he was set. He rummaged through his backpack that was in a state of disarray. *Where is it? It can't be gone. I desperately need to get some more practice in before the competition in three days.* After digging through the heaps of clothes that littered the floor and hastily sorting through the crumpled paper strewn across his desk, Jai finally realized that he had lent it to Randy at school. Just as Jai was beginning to panic, he remembered that his nanna had given him a calculator in that Medley of Talents box.

Jai raced to Veer's room and barged in through the door, purposefully ignoring the Do Not Enter sign. Maneuvering through the minefield of clothes piles, he made his way to Veer's bed. Jai sorted through all of the miscellaneous items stuffed under his brother's bed until he found the familiar wooden box. All that was left inside now was the sleek black graphing calculator. Jai grabbed it and headed back to his room, eager to finish off one of Mr. Steel's problems. Once he returned to his room, he started to plug in the long list of numbers that comprised the statistics problem. A couple of minutes later, he pushed Enter and waited for the calculator to do its job. What it spit out was far from what Jai expected. The calculator read "21 + 0." *That's strange.* Just to make sure that calculator was functioning properly, Jai plugged in a couple of simple addition problems. But again and again, the calculator continued to return "21 + 0." Then the realization hit him. *Of course, how could I be so stupid!* Just like all of the other items from the box, the calculator was nonfunctional. But if Jai's hunch was right, that meant something else as well. *Another clue!*

Just as they were beginning to lose hope after no new revelations about Samir's whereabouts another clue had surfaced! Jai immediately called up Veer and Vidya. A meeting was necessary. Immediately.

Jai quickly grabbed the calculator and stealthily slipped it in his coat pocket, as he was aware that bugs could still be hidden around the house. Then he casually sauntered outside, appearing as if he were going on an afternoon stroll. As he strode along the driveway, he thought he saw a black silhouette perched in the tall tree in their front yard. But when he glanced in its direction, the tree was vacant apart from a noisy family of squirrels. *Maybe I'm just being paranoid.* Jai brushed it off. Yet he still took no chances and kept the same leisurely walking pace all the way to Vidya's house, even though he felt like sprinting as fast as he could to reveal the news to Veer and Vidya. Once he reached the top floor of the apartment building, Vidya answered the door.

"You're not going to believe what I'm about to tell you," Jai said immediately.

"What could possibly be exciting, Jai?" Vidya asked uncaringly. Vidya was usually the cheerful one out of the trio, and she was the last one to give up hope. Nevertheless, Vidya was starting to feel the disappointment over the lack of meaningful clues.

"I found one," he replied and by her reaction, Jai knew that she understood what he was getting at. She shrieked excitedly and jumped up into the air.

"I can't believe it! After you guys told me about 'Faize,' I didn't think there would be another clue!" After she was done expressing her excitement, she started barraging Jai with questions. "How did you find it? Do you know what it means? Where did it come from?"

"We have to wait until Veer gets here, then I'll tell you guys everything.

As if on cue, Veer showed up, sweating heavily. "Jai, why did you call me up now? I was just at the Rec Center about to beat my bench press record. What's the big deal?"

"I found another clue," Jai answered calmly.

"What? Are you sure?"

"One hundred percent."

"Yes!" Veer seemed even more excited than Vidya, if that was possible. "Do you know what it means?"

"We're going to need to decipher it first. Hopefully, it will shed some light on the meanings of the other clues also."

But as much as they researched and brainstormed, the trio yielded no answers. Jai was beginning to think that they wouldn't be able to solve the clues. *After five clues, we still don't have any idea where Nanna is. Maybe it's too late. Maybe he is already gone . . .*

Today was the day. This was the first thought that entered Veer's head as he opened his eyes in the morning. Almost a year's worth of training, and all of it came down to this day, the Medley of Talents competition. Already the nerves were getting to him. He could feel his stomach churning and already beads of sweat were starting to appear on his forehead. Veer tried to remain as calm as possible, thinking of all the practice he had done over the past year, but it just made him all the more nervous.

When Veer descended the stairs, he could tell that his brother was just as apprehensive about the competition. Jai sat still, staring blankly at an untouched bowl of cereal.

"Hey, Jai, snap out of it! If we're going to win this competition, you've got to eat up. You can't run on an empty stomach." Jai barely looked up to acknowledge his brother, and then returned to staring at his bowl of cereal as if it were the strangest thing he'd ever seen. "Come on, Jai, you know that Nanna wanted us to win this."

"Nanna's not here, Veer. And he never will be."

Veer was nearly brought to tears by his brother's blunt statement. "How can you just give up like that?" he yelled back angrily.

"We haven't found anything useful! Nanna didn't give us any clues. He just gave us a bunch of broken stuff."

Veer had now regained his composure. "Even if Nanna isn't here, wouldn't you want to make him proud by winning Medley of Talents?"

Jai said nothing and started to shovel down his cereal. Veer knew that deep inside, Jai wanted to make Samir proud more than anything.

The bus ride to school was silent. It seemed as if everyone was just as nervous as Jai and Veer over the competition, including Vidya. Usually in June, kids were buzzing over the prospect of no more school for three months. But not today. The Medley of Talents competition was the only thought that filled their heads.

Once the students got off the bus, they were told to go to their respective homerooms. In the ten minutes before they had to be in class, Veer called a quick team meeting.

"All right guys, I know we're all nervous and I think that everyone else is too," Veer said. *And by the looks of it, that includes Jed, Sid, and Gavin,* Veer thought to himself as he saw the three bullies' pale faces. Normally they would be stuffing some poor kid into a locker, but today they were just moving along with the rest of the crowd. "But I really think we have a shot at this."

Jai and Vidya both agreed.

"Does everyone have what they need for the competition?"

"Yup, I have a pen and paper. That's all I need," Vidya responded.

"I've got my calculator for the math competition and running shoes for the race," Jai said.

"And I've got my guitar for the music competition. I think we're set," Veer finished. "Good luck, guys."

Ten minutes later, Veer, Jai, and Vidya were standing amongst a thousand students in the small school gymnasium. The entire school was packed into the room anxiously waiting for Mr. Harrison's speech. Standing in a large rowdy middle school crowd was an unpleasant experience for Veer, Jai, and Vidya, but they were too focused on the competition to care. After five more long restless minutes, Mr. Harrison's stocky figure finally appeared on the podium.

"Sorry for the delay," he began, his familiar gruff voice with a thick New York accent booming through the speakers. Veer couldn't help but think of how little Mr. Harrison did for their team as a Medley of Talents coach. Every single time they tried to schedule a meeting with him, he always seemed to be busy. *Actually, the only time he even met with us was when he gave us that wooden box.* Veer remembered the box filled with the seemingly unsolvable clues bitterly. "Welcome one and all to the first annual Medley of Talents competition," Mr. Harrison continued.

"Sounds like something from a corny TV show." A voice from somewhere next to him snickered.

"Yeah, can we get on with it already?" another voice yelled.

But as usual, Mr. Harrison explained the rules for the thousandth time, even though they had been drilled into all of the students' heads throughout the school year. Then he went on to talk about the sportsmanship award and go into every detail about the competition. After a long speech, Mr. Harrison finally ended with a dramatic, "Let the games begin!"

Veer sat backstage, anxiously anticipating the first out of five Medley events, the music competition. Veer calmed himself and closed his eyes. He could hear the powerful notes of his song flowing through his head and almost feel his fingers flying over the smooth neck of his electric guitar. One by one he listened to the beautiful and smooth melodies performed by the students before him, and with each successive one, his apprehension grew. Veer was beginning to realize that everyone had performed a classical song, making the rock ballad that he wrote either unique, or out of place. But the big question was: which way would the judges see it?

"Veer Gupta." A low booming voice sounded over the microphone. Veer froze when he heard his name, and it felt as if frigid ice filled his veins. *This is it. Here I go.* Veer lugged his large guitar amplifier and his beloved guitar onto stage. Immediately by the judges' reactions, he knew it wasn't what they expected. *This is either really good, or really bad.*

After he set everything up, Veer stepped up to the microphone and cleared his throat. "My piece is called Inferno." He was beginning to sense that the judges were unsettled. *Oh well, I'll just have impress them with my playing.*

Veer began with a simple power chord and let its deep notes resonate throughout the gymnasium. Then his fingers slid over to the base of the neck and began to fly over the strings, just as he had imagined. He hit every note with precise rhythm, and his song was beginning to take shape. After he had hit every note perfectly in the intro, he began the chorus. Veer's fingers rapidly contorted in order to play every chord with his expert accuracy that he had attained through painstaking hours of practice. His right hand strummed up and down steadily upon the six strings of his guitar. Veer was nearing the end of his song, which he had performed flawlessly up until this point. *Now it's time for the improvised solo.* Veer's fingers once again slid over to the base of the neck, where he could hit all of the high notes. Then he just let his fingers loose and they ran wild. Veer incorporated all types of techniques into the solo, including bends, slides, and trills, making this solo the true masterpiece of the song. One minute and dozens of notes later, Veer was taking a bow and receiving thunderous applause. *That was awesome! Even if the judges don't think so, everyone else knows that no one else can top that,* Veer thought confidently.

But the competition was not over yet. There still was one more contestant, Gavin. As soon as he walked on stage with a smirk on his face, Veer knew that he was going to give a tough fight. And he did.

He sat down at his drums and pulled out two drumsticks from his sleeves, yelling with ferocity. *It's all just drama.* Gavin started off with a steady drum roll that gradually grew faster. Then he broke into a rhythm, all of his limbs working the drums with perfect coordination. Finally, there was the solo. Gavin's hands were pounding the drums so fast and hard that all that could be seen was a fantastic blur. By the end, Gavin had worked up a huge sweat and he was pumping his fist as the crowd cheered his name. Gavin had matched or even surpassed Veer. Veer knew that it was going to be a long day.

Vidya took deep breaths and watched herself twirl her pen in between her fingers. *This is my one event, and I need to make it count.* After seeing Gavin's amazing drum solo, Vidya realized that she desperately needed to win her writing event if they wanted to hold the Medley trophy at the end of the day. She watched the proctor's mouth moving as he explained the rules that she had already memorized, but his words did not register, for Vidya's mind was elsewhere.

What will the prompt be? Are they going to make us write prose or poetry? None of her questions would be answered until she turned over the piece of paper in front of her.

Suddenly Sid's annoying voice interrupted her train of thought. "Hey, I dropped my pen, could you get it for me?" Vidya looked to her right to see Sid's sneering face. She rolled her eyes and put her own pen down on her desk. As she bent down to grab Sid's pen, Vidya felt something brush against her head. When she sat back down after returning his pen, she was shocked to see her own pen that was sitting on her desk a few seconds earlier, missing. Vidya immediately knew where it had gone. She looked over to her right to see Sid sneering back at her and mockingly trying to twirl her pen. He mouthed a single word at her: sucker.

Vidya was filled with rage. *He stole my pen and I can't do anything about it. The competition is about to start!* She was even more worried when she recalled her English teacher telling her that without her materials, she would be disqualified from the competition. She couldn't even ask the proctor for one. Her mind was just beginning to race with anxiety when she gladly remembered that she packed an extra pen in the morning just to be on the safe side. *That was close.*

"Your time begins now." Vidya flipped over the paper to see a single sentence at the top.

"Describe the most beautiful place in the world."

Usually when Vidya read the prompt, immediately a myriad of ideas would flow through her head and she would frantically scribble them all down. Then she would piece them together later. But now her mind was absolutely blank. Nothing. It was as if a vacuum were sucking the thoughts right out of her head. All she saw in her mind's eye was a blank screen. No pictures, faces, or sounds. Absolutely nothing. *Writer's block.*

With thirty minutes over and only half the time left, Vidya's paper was still blank. All around her, the other contestants had already filled up their pages and were editing their pieces. *How can I let down Veer and Jai? I had to win this, and I still don't have a single word down.* Vidya was beginning to feel tears well up in her eyes. *And worst of all, how can I let Uncle down?* An image of Veer and Jai's father flashed through her mind's eye.

Then a raging river of thoughts obliterated the dam of the writer's block. Suddenly memories started to pour through her head. She was with Veer, Jai, and Samir in their backyard. Golden light illuminated all of their smiling faces. All around her she heard laughter. *That's it! The most beautiful place in the world: home.* The words of her piece instantaneously started to course through her pen on to the blank sheet of paper and five minutes later, she had nearly filled up the entire page.

After Vidya had read through her piece two more times and edited it thoroughly, she was satisfied. *And just in time,* she thought to herself as she watched the second hand of the clock tick down for the last ten seconds.

"All right, all writers put your pens down and hand your paper to the front."

As she passed her paper to the front, she glanced over at Sid. He was snickering in the corner with one of his friends as he pointed at her. Vidya squinted her eyes and returned a cold hard stare. *Fine, if they want to cheat, if that's how they want to play it, we'll still beat them.*

The loud raucous noise of the cafeteria filled Veer's ears as he searched for Jai and Vidya among the lunching middle school students. Finally he spotted Vidya's face in the back of the large cafeteria. Veer bobbed and weaved through the throng of students with expertise after navigating crowds for the past year. Once he reached their table, he could see that Vidya's normal cheerful expression had changed to that of pure anger.

"What's wrong?" Veer asked. "I thought we did pretty well so far today."

"It's not that. I think that Sid's team is cheating."

"What?"

"I wouldn't put it past them," Jai chimed in as he joined them at the table.

"But, it didn't look like Gavin was cheating during the music competition," Veer argued.

"Well, Sid sure cheated during the writing competition. He stole my pen and attempted to get me disqualified," Vidya retorted.

"Wow. We better watch out," Jai responded.

"Yeah, we still have three events left. We should just avoid them for the rest of the day," Veer said.

"At least the next three events aren't subject to the judges' opinions," Vidya pointed out.

"True. We have to try to win all of them though, because then it's a sure bet to win the whole thing." Jai summed up the team's goal.

"Easier said than done," Veer said grimly. "Sid beat my pull-up record before. Who says he isn't going to beat me in arm wrestling?"

"I believe in you, Veer." Jai tried to instill confidence in his brother. "You've got this one."

Let's hope I do, Veer thought to himself as he took a bite of the gourmet sandwich that his mousi had packed for him. The rest of lunch was eaten in silence as the trio anxiously anticipated the three remaining Medley events.

Jai stared down at a sheet of paper with five math problems on it. He looked up at the clock that read "1:25." That meant he only had five minutes left for the remaining problem. The first four problems had been math brainteasers, just like the ones he received in Mr. Steel's class. Usually Jai would immediately have several ideas flow through his head about how to solve Mr. Steel's brainteasers, but today his mind was blank. He couldn't believe the pressure was getting to him. He looked down at his scratch paper, which was full of crossed out symbols and numbers and covered with eraser dust. He had tried at least a dozen different methods to solve the previous problem, and after ten minutes of struggling, he found the answer.

Jai gulped. Usually the last problem was the hardest in math competitions, and he expected Medley of Talents to be the same. He read the fifth problem over and over, and nothing came to him. His mind started to race. Others, like Hal, were definitely going to answer the first four problems correctly, if not the fifth. Veer and Vidya had been counting on him to win the math competition, and he couldn't let them down. He looked up at the clock, and the second hand seemed to be moving faster than ever. Now he only had four minutes. Jai was panicking.

Jai read the problem one more time, and miraculously, he figured out how to solve the problem. He just needed to punch a couple of keys on his calculator and he would be set. Jai grabbed his calculator from the corner of his desk and started punching the buttons as fast as he could. But nothing appeared on the screen. He jammed his finger on the "ON" button, but still the screen remained blank. *What's going on?*

Jai flipped over his calculator and opened up the battery compartment. It was empty. *I am one hundred percent sure that I put in new batteries this morning.* Then he heard a derisive snort from across the room. He glanced over to see Gavin's mocking face and four AA batteries in his chubby fingers. Jai was filled with hot anger as he pictured Gavin holding the Medley of Talents trophy. *I can't let these cheaters win.*

Jai looked up at the clock again. There were only two and a half minutes left. His brain kicked into high gear. *I may just have enough time to solve this problem by hand, but I can't make a single mistake.* He began furiously scribbling numbers down on the page of scratch paper while performing mental calculations as fast as he could. Halfway down the page, his mechanical pencil broke under his tight grip and a thin piece of lead fell out. *Everything is going wrong now.* But nothing was going to stop Jai at this point. He grabbed the thin piece of lead with his bare hand and continued writing.

"Ten seconds remaining," the proctor called. Jai was almost there.

"Five, four, three, two, one." Jai jotted down his answer on the problem sheet. "Pencils down. Please pass your papers up."

Jai looked at the scratch paper covered with his messy handwriting. All he could do now was hope that he hadn't made a mistake.

As soon as Jai stepped out onto the track, he felt the intense heat of the summer sun beating down upon him. He felt confident, as he had gotten much faster since he had set the school record for the mile run at the beginning of the year. He looked over to see hundreds of anxious faces in the stands, and heard his name being called several times. But he was too focused on one thing to process any of it: solely the Medley of Talents race.

Mr. Harrison's gruff voice erupted over the loudspeaker. "All runners, the first event is the one-hundred-meter run. It will be run in a tournament-like fashion. The top six qualifiers will move on to the second stage of the running event, the mile run."

After everyone in the audience had taken their seats, the blaring loudspeaker sounded once again. "All right, first heat of runners up. On your marks, get set, go!" Heat after heat passed by, until Jai finally heard his name among the list of runners.

Jai lined up with the other runners and set his feet in the starting blocks. As soon as the sound of the gunshot echoed through the air, Jai was off in a flash. He pumped his arms rapidly as he pushed off each leg with explosive power. Halfway into the race, he was already thirty meters ahead of the closest competitor, and expanding his lead quickly. Jai continued to accelerate, pushing himself to the very limit until he finally rocketed past the finish line.

"Ten point five seconds," Mr. Randolph called out.

Jai coasted to a stop, as the crowd roared with excitement. He had beaten the previous leader, Jed, by two and a half seconds, which seems like a century in a sprint. Jai could not stop himself from letting out a victorious shout. After the crowd had died down in anticipation of then next heat of runners, Jai was looking ahead to the next portion of the competition. *I can't get too confident. I've still got to win the mile run.*

After three more uneventful heats, the second phase of the competition was finally set to start. Jai closed his eyes to find tranquility and comfort in his meditation-like state. Yet soon his trance was broken by a condescending voice.

"Hey, good luck on the race." Jed's lanky figure came into Jai's view. As one of the top six finishers in the short distance portion, he also had a shot at winning the long distance title. "You're goanna need it," Jed whispered into Jai's ear. The bully then stomped on Jai's foot and twisted.

Immediately, white-hot pain shot up Jai's leg. He fell to the ground, clasping his ankle and rocking back and forth on his back. *How could I be so stupid and let him cheat?*

The other runners, including Randy, helped Jai to his feet.

"Are you okay?" Randy asked.

"Yeah, man, I'm fine. Just don't let anyone know that I'm hurt, or they won't let me race."

"You sure?" Randy asked.

"Runners on your marks." Mr. Harrison on the loudspeaker cut him off. *I've got no choice if I want to win,* Jai thought to himself as he hobbled over to the starting line. "Get set." A waiting period of a few nerve-racking seconds elapsed. Then finally Mr. Harrison shouted, "Go!"

Jai pushed off his left noninjured leg, then sped off to fight to take the lead in the first half-lap. He took long hard strides with his left leg and landed sprightly on his right. Once he took the lead in the first half-lap, the pain in his leg started to numb. Jai began to speed up the pace until the only person who could match him was Jed, with his long loping strides.

"You're going down, Gupta!" Jed said through gritted teeth and between breaths.

"In your dreams, Jed." Jai bolted ahead to complete the first lap, leaving Jed in the dust. With the adrenaline coursing through his veins, Jai was able to keep up the same incredible pace throughout the second of four laps. But by the time the third lap rolled around, he could start to feel the pain creeping back into his ankle. The pain gradually increased with each step until it was almost unbearable half way through the third lap. To make the situation worse, Jed was gaining on him. When they passed Mr. Randolph for the third time, Jed and Jai were neck and neck.

Jai heard Veer and Vidya calling his name and just knew he had to bear the pain for one more lap. Perspiration soaked his shirt and he was beginning to feel his injured leg shake from exhaustion. Yet Jed was matching him all the way through. With two hundred meters left of the race, Jai was struggling to keep up.

"See ya, Gupta!" Jed yelled as he shot ahead with an extra burst of speed that he had been saving up for the end. *How can I lose after all that training? Even worse, how can I let everyone down?* Pictures of Vidya, Veer, and his amma flashed through his head. Then there was his nanna.

It was as if a spark went off in Jai's body, and energy poured back into him. The memory of Samir ignited the flame and Jai bounded ahead. Even with Jai's resurgence, Jed was still fifty meters ahead with only a short distance remaining to the finish line. Jai pushed himself to the very limit even though his body was screaming for him to stop. He finally was tied with Jed with ten meters to go. *Come on!* Jai exploded off his left leg and that put him a half-body length ahead. But then Jed leaped a bit further, reversing the situation. With less than five meters to go, Jai stuck his neck forward and jumped.

His world was enveloped into darkness as Jai hit the ground. Pure exhaustion led Jai to collapse. He embraced his restful sleep until it was soon interrupted by a constant tapping on his shoulders.

"Jai! Wake up!" Jai awoke greeted by Veer and Vidya's faces. He slowly rose from the rubbery track floor, caressing a now hugely swollen ankle.

"Congrats, bro!" Veer slapped his brother on the back so hard that Jai almost fell back down to the floor. "Oops, my bad."

"You won!" Vidya exclaimed as she helped Jai to his feet. As Jai moved back toward the school, half-limping and half being carried by the crowd, he felt that incredible feeling of accomplishment welling up in his chest.

June sunlight poured through the large gymnasium windows and illuminated the stage of the final Medley competition, arm-wrestling. The sun's blazing heat along with the body warmth of a thousand anxious students made the room feel like an oven. Yet, Veer felt as if he was stuck in the middle of a blizzard, for the chills in anticipation of competition were getting to him. He could feel the goose bumps erupting over his entire body as the competitors streamed in one after another.

When the last competitor entered the gymnasium, Veer's anxiety was replaced with a burning desire to win. Once he spotted Sid with his typical demeaning grin spread across his face, Veer knew he had to beat the bully. But the wise voice in Veer's head peeped up. *But I can't let my grudge against Sid get in the way of winning the competition. I've got to play it smart and stay focused.*

The preliminary rounds of the arm-wrestling competition flew by. One after another, he slammed his competitor's fist to the table with virtually no resistance.

With three rounds finished, Veer had efficiently dispatched all three of his competitors without even breaking a sweat.

Before the fifth round began, Veer glanced over at Sid's table. It looked as if he was finishing off his competitors without even trying. Sid was yawning when the next competitor walked up, who was a bulky eighth grader. Sid leaned back in the chair and locked hands with his opponent. In less than a second, the hefty kid's hand was pinned painfully against the table, and Sid's face lit up with his menacing grin.

After two more blowout rounds, both Veer and Sid had reached the finals. As the judges set up the table, Jai ran over from the stands to give his brother a pep talk.

"Hey, Veer, you've got this. This is what you've been training months for," Jai said, continually poking his brother in the chest. Veer half-listened to his brother's motivational speech, but his focus drifted toward Sid, who was laughing alongside Jed and Gavin. "Hey!" Jai smacked Veer on the head.

"What was that for?"

"Don't worry about him. This is all about you, no pressure, Veer. Just go up there and do what you have been doing for the past seven rounds." With that Jai left to the stands.

A booming voice on the loudspeaker called Veer and Sid to the center table, where the final match was being held. Veer closed his eyes and took a deep breath. He listened to the cheers of the crowd and felt his confidence building up. There was no way that Sid was going to beat him this time.

But before Veer could even open his eyes, he felt an incredible pain shooting through his right shoulder. The first image he saw was Sid's menacing grin. Veer collapsed against the wall, and could feel the world spinning around him. He could barely make out Gavin's chunky figure slipping back into the crowd and the glint of shiny brass on his knuckles.

CHAPTER 11

Veer grasped his shoulder and doubled over. His entire arm dangled helplessly in midair as he rapidly sucked in air. *This can't stop me.* The pain was intensifying. *I have got to win.* As Veer closed his eyes in efforts to ignore the pain, his mind flashed back to two years ago.

It was the finals of his recreational basketball tournament and his team was down by one with ten seconds left. Samir, who was also Veer and Jai's coach at the time, had called one last time out.

"Veer, you're the point guard, and the only one who can lead us to victory. Do you see that basket?" Samir faced Veer toward their basket. "You can't let anything get in the way between you and that basket. That basket is victory."

Veer looked over at the opposing team and gulped nervously. "I . . . I don't think I can do it, Nanna. I'll just let the whole team down. Why can't you just let someone else on our team do it?"

"No!" Veer was surprised with the amount of force that was in Samir's voice. "Veer, you can do it. I believe in you."

Then suddenly Veer was back in the gymnasium of Medley Middle. He could hear the crowd screaming, and his shoulder hurting even more than before. But it didn't matter because now he was convinced. Nothing could come in the way of victory!

Veer walked toward the table with his eyes fixed on one person, Sid. He was smiling even more than before now, his grin spreading from ear to ear. *He knows I'm hurt and he is going to try to take advantage of it.*

Once Veer was seated at the table, the judges called for the competitors to shake hands before the arm-wrestling match started in the act of sportsmanship.

"Good luck, Veer," Sid said. "I know we're going to have a great match." Then Sid slapped Veer on the right shoulder, squarely where Gavin had injured before, with an unnecessary amount of force.

Veer's shoulder was deluged with an almost unbearable amount of pain. But he held it all in, and managed a smile back at Sid.

The judge for the final match was Mr. Randolph. Like a drill sergeant, he began to bellow out orders. "We will begin the competition with the left hand arm-wrestling match. Competitors lock your hands."

Veer's hand was enveloped by Sid's crushing grip.

"Begin!"

Sid immediately snapped his wrist so Veer's hand was contorted into a painful position. Then Sid pressed down until Veer felt as if his wrist was about to shatter into a million pieces. Not only was his wrist about to break, but also Veer was losing ground. His hand was slowly being forced toward the table as Sid was beginning to press down with even greater force. But all Veer could do was smile. *I think it's time to take you down, Sid.*

Veer clenched his hand and rotated his wrist back into normal position. Then with ease, he flexed his left forearm and rapidly turned his shoulder. In an instant, the situation was flipped with Sid now at a disadvantage. Now, Veer simply overpowered Sid, making him slowly lose inch by inch. Sid's face was beginning to turn red. With one final mighty effort, Veer smashed Sid's hand against the table. *I feel even stronger than before!*

Mr. Randolph blew the whistle. Once again, he began shouting in a gruff voice, "Winner of the left hand round is Veer Gupta. Now, we will commence the right hand arm-wrestling match."

Sid immediately recovered from his defeat and began to smile. "Now its time for the real match. You know you're going to lose Gupta."

In spite of Veer's bitter rivalry with Sid, he kept his calm. "We'll see."

Once more, the two competitors locked hands. Now Veer's shoulder was hurting more than ever, with even a slight twitch sending searing pain throughout his arm.

"Begin!"

This time Sid did not even try to hurt Veer's wrist, but instead went straight for his injured right shoulder by contorting Veer's forearm. Veer grimaced and yelped in pain. Sid continued to bend Veer's forearm, laughing maniacally. Now Veer felt as if his entire right arm was on fire with pain flooding all of his senses. *Fight through it!* Veer's hand was less than an inch away from the table. Sid continued to put immense pressure on Veer's right hand. *I'm going to lose.*

But as Veer's hand was nearing the table, he remembered all of the training he had done just to prepare for a moment like this. *I've got to fight back!* Veer began pushing upward with all his might. Yet the harder Veer tried, he was met by even more pain. *Nothing can get in the way of victory.* Veer battled through his pain and continued to muscle his way back into the match. Now Veer had almost pushed Sid back to the halfway point, and he could see beads of sweat pouring down Sid's face. *He's getting tired, but my shoulder can't hold up much longer. Time is no friend to either of us.*

Veer finally battled his way back to where he started. But when he tried to push Sid's hand even further, Sid was unrelenting. The two remained in a deadlock for what seemed like an eternity. After a long thirty seconds, Veer could feel his shoulder about to give way.

Just as Veer was about to slip again, he heard the crowd's cheers. Then he heard Vidya and Jai shouting, and knew he could not let them down. A second wave of energy crashed upon him and surged through his veins. It also numbed his pain to a bearable amount. Veer then poured all of that energy into his arm and rotated his shoulder with an amazing amount of torque. Sid tried to fight back, but Veer's power was just too much for him. Finally, Sid's hand was slammed against the table. The crowd went wild.

Veer spotted Jai and Vidya's faces among the huge sea of students sitting in the bleachers and ran up to join them. Along the way dozens of students swarmed around him, shaking his hand and congratulating him for winning the arm-wrestling competition. After a long trip up, Veer finally found his way to his two best friends.

"I told you that you could do it, Veer. You won!" Jai patted his brother on the back.

"That was awesome, Veer!" Vidya squealed excitedly. "I just hope I can say the same about my writing."

But before Veer could respond, Mr. Harrison silenced the crowd. His gruff New York accent echoed throughout the gymnasium. "Finally, after a full year's preparation, the

Medley of Talents competition has come to a close. I can't tell you how proud I am about how the competition was held. All the competitors were true sportsmen."

"Yeah right," Veer muttered sarcastically. "You had blatant cheaters right in front of your eyes."

"And everyone tried their hardest," Mr. Harrison continued. Then the principal went on to discuss how the competition represented a well-rounded individual and good moral character. But to the middle school students, Mr. Harrison could be reading the phone book for all they cared. His dull and monotonous speech continued until finally the rowdiest of the bunch spoke up.

"Hey, can we get to the results?" Jed yelled out from the crowd. A chorus of agreement followed from the entire crowd.

"All right, all right." Mr. Harrison submitted. He walked over to the judges' table to retrieve the results. Veer, Jai, and Vidya huddled together in nervous anticipation.

"Okay, guys. We know we have won the running event and the arm-wrestling competition for sure, which may mean we have already won," Jai said. "But we can't be sure, because another team could have possibly won all of the other three events. Keep your hopes up, and even if we didn't win, we know we've tried our best." Veer and Vidya nodded in agreement, but all that the trio could think of was the feeling of holding the first-place trophy in their hands.

"After long deliberation over both the writing and music competitions, the winner is . . ." Mr. Harrison paused for an unnecessarily long amount of time. The students started a drum roll to add to the anticipation even more. Veer was so nervous that he could not stop himself from shaking. "Group 14: Veer and Jai Gupta, and Vidya

Reddy! They did a clean-sweep, winning all five Medley competitions!"

As soon as they heard their names, the trio jumped up from the stands. Vidya screamed happily the entire time, while Veer whooped in excitement. Jai just stood still with a smile on his face. They had won it all.

After the excitement had died down, Mr. Harrison continued, "Will the winners please come down to claim the prize?" The trio walked down the stands to the podium with their heads held high. "Due to reasons which don't concern you, we have decided to change the prize this year. The champion group will get an all-expense paid trip to the Museum of Science and Technology located at Twenty-first Street and O Avenue in Washington DC."

While the rest of the students were booing about how lame the prize was, Jai suddenly remembered something. *The last clue!*

CHAPTER 12

"**S**o you're saying that the 21 + 0 meant that Uncle was trying to send us to the National Museum of Science and Technology?" Vidya asked while munching on a bajji, an Indian snack consisting of a fried spicy batter covering vegetables. The trio was back at Vidya's apartment after the Medley ceremony, utterly surprised about Jai's breakthrough.

"I guess. This was also the last of the five clues in the box, meaning that the only way that we'll figure out any more is by going to the museum."

"But why the museum?" Veer wondered as he reached for another bajji. "How does it have anything to do with Nanna's disappearance?"

"Well, why don't we rehash the clues we have got so far?" Vidya proposed logically. "I found the anagram in the fountain pen. That led us to Basketball Battle, which finally led us to Dr. Juarez."

"But he gave us no useful information and we ended up at a dead end," Jai said pessimistically. "But when I was running outside, Veer noticed the word Virus on the stopwatch Nanna gave me."

"But again, that didn't lead us anywhere," Veer continued. "Then Jai helped me discover that the number of pounds in each of my weights was the same as the numbers of our basketball jerseys. Those led us to our old basketball, which had the word Faize written on us."

"Yeah, and Veer you found another clue didn't you?" Jai asked.

"Mmhm, my guitar tuner read out the notes Gaffa."

"Then finally, I found the 21+ 0 on my calculator."

"So Dr. Juarez, virus, Gaffa, Faize, and the National Museum of Science and Technology," Vidya pondered. "We don't even know what two of them mean, and what do the other three have to do with each other?"

"I guess we'll just have to find out at the museum," Veer responded.

Sunlight radiated down upon Washington DC as Veer, Jai, and Vidya exited Anu's station wagon at Twenty-first Street and O Avenue on Saturday morning. Veer mopped the perspiration that was already building up on his brow as the trio headed toward the museum that looked like something out of a science fiction novel. As they approached the building, the trio noticed a huge crowd of people growing outside of the museum entrance.

"What's all of this about?" Jai wondered.

Vidya was the first to spot the small sign posted above the museum doors. "They are unveiling a new exhibit today. But it seems as if it's sold out, and now they're turning a bunch of people down for tickets."

Veer glanced down at the tickets that were their "prize" for winning the Medley of Talents competition. They read: Valid for All Exhibits. "Hey, guys, guess what? These tickets are actually useful, they'll get us into the exhibit."

"All right, let's check it out," Vidya said excitedly.

The trio darted in and out of the crowd in front of the museum, now proficient in weaving through large crowds of people after traversing the jam-packed middle school hallways. Finally, they caught sight of the museum doors and squirmed through. Immediately, a cold gust of air-conditioned air soothed the trio after the blistering June weather.

After the long wait through security, they finally reached the main attraction. The sign read "The Deadliest Disease the World Has Ever Seen: Finally a Cure." Then underneath it, printed in bold "sponsored by Vaccine Corporation, saving the world one cure at a time."

"That's the company that Amma works at!" Veer exclaimed.

The trio stepped inside the exhibit, and immediately they were in awe. Reporters and news cameras were set up on almost every possible inch not taken up by the exhibit, leaving virtually no space for the enormous crowd. Once they entered, a loud voice sounded from the speakers, "The speech will begin in ten minutes, please enjoy the exhibit in the meantime."

Veer, Jai, and Vidya weaved through the crowd to the center of the exhibit. Standing there was a giant metallic structure, consisting of a polyhedron with eight spidery legs branching off.

"What is it?" Veer wondered aloud.

He was answered when the plaque at the bottom of the statue came into view through the huge mass of people. It read "The most destructive virus to date, the Gaffa virus."

The realization hit Veer. "Jai! Vidya! It's the Gaffa virus! Those were two of Nanna's clues!"

Vidya's eyes were wide in amazement. "So Uncle was trying to lead us here all along."

"But we still don't have an idea of what he is trying to tell us," Jai said realistically. "Let's look around some more and see if we can try to piece it together."

But Veer was already way ahead of him. "Hey, guys, over here!" Veer motioned from the opposite side of the Gaffa structure. Jai and Vidya threaded their way through the crowd and reporters until they finally reached the sign that Veer was standing in front of.

On top was a grotesque photograph of a man infected with the Gaffa virus. His face was so disfigured with inflamed lesions that he was barely recognizable as human. His mouth was coated with froth and his limbs were so skinny that they could not have been much more than just skin and bone. Vidya was so shocked when she saw the picture that she turned away in tears.

"I know," Veer said acknowledging the picture. "But keep reading."

"The man above has been infected with the Gaffa virus. Known symptoms include internal bleeding, widespread inflammation, a high fever of at least 105 degrees Fahrenheit, paralysis, seizures, and certain death in less than a day. But symptoms vary from case to case because of the virus's ability to mutate at a high rate and accomplish what no organism has done before. The virus seems to adapt to the specific case to attack that specific person's weakest point. If the Gaffa virus were to spread, consequences would be catastrophic, and it could possibly wipe out the human population as we know it. But luckily, the Gaffa virus was restricted to a rural South Indian village named Patnam. And fortunately after studying these cases, the hard-working doctors at Vaccine Corp. risked their lives and developed a cure . . ."

"Patnam!" Jai realized. "That's the village that Dr. Juarez mentioned!"

The speakers boomed once more. "Would everyone please gather around the podium, the speech is about to begin." The massive crowd converged and the trio darted toward the front. "Would the crowd please welcome Vaccine Corporation's representative here at the National Museum for Science and Technology, Dr. Nathaniel Faize!" While the thunderous applause was echoing, Veer, Jai, and Vidya exchanged shocked glances. A fit-looking old man stepped up to the podium. In spite of his age, the man kept a strong posture.

"A few years ago, I visited a children's school in Patnam, a small village in India," he began in a powerful confident voice. "I can still remember the smiles on the children's faces even when their families were stricken with poverty and they had less than a single meal a day. Yet, they were delighted to meet even a stranger." He paused to scan the crowd. "Two years ago, a disease struck Patnam. Those innocent children were dead in less than a day." Gasps and cries echoed from the crowd. "The culprit was the Gaffa virus." Dr. Faize gestured at the giant sculpture behind him. "They had no chance against this monster. Most of the town's population was wiped out. Officials were notified, but it was already too late, for the virus kills in a few hours. To prevent widespread panic, the media hasn't been notified until now," he continued. "But luckily, the danger has already passed." Sighs of relief came from almost every person in the crowd. "This is a result of the hard work from the scientists at Vaccine Corp. They risked their lives and entered the danger zone, the village of Patnam, to collect samples of the Gaffa virus. Then they labored day and night without rest to find ways to beat the bug, but the virus seemed insurmountable. Everything they threw at it was rendered useless in a matter of minutes because of the virus's unbelievably high mutation rate. Yet, as I have always said, the human mind can accomplish anything. Just recently, the labor of the gifted minds of our scientists came to fruition." He added a dramatic pause. "We have found a cure!"

Deafening applause came from the enormous crowd. But while overenthusiastic crowd members around them were screaming at the top of their lungs, the trio was baffled. *Where is Nanna trying to lead us?* Veer wondered.

"Thank you, thank you!" Dr. Faize gestured for the crowd to quiet down. "I will now take questions." Immediately, the hands of every single reporter in the room shot up into the air. But before Dr. Faize could single out a reporter from the sea of hands, one of the security officers from behind the podium came out to whisper something into his ears.

The security officer was a giant of a man, towering over Dr. Faize who was standing on the podium. He had striking blue eyes that stood out on his enormous body rippling with muscle. As Dr. Faize responded, the man brought up his hand to scratch a clean-shaven head. Then Veer saw it. A deep scar that ran down the man's hand sparked his memory. *He must be the one who tried to strangle Jai!*

Veer whispered frantically to convey his discovery to Jai and Vidya.

"Are you sure?" Jai whispered back.

"One hundred percent." Then the realization hit the trio simultaneously.

"Then that can mean only one thing." Jai gulped. "Vaccine Corp. has been attacking us!"

There was no time for the shock to settle in. The bodyguards behind Dr. Faize were staring straight in the direction of Veer, Jai, and Vidya. They began to converge through the crowd toward the trio. "And they're about to do it again," Vidya whispered anxiously.

CHAPTER 13

"**V**idya, Jai, run!" Veer yelled. "I'll fend them off!"

The bodyguards were now only a few feet away. Veer was paralyzed by the large bodyguard's piercing blue gaze. Just as the man was closing in, Jai grabbed Veer by his shirt collar.

"No, we're sticking as a group!" Jai hissed into his ear. Veer shook himself out of his trance. "Hold onto my shoulder."

With Vidya in the lead and Veer bringing up the rear, the trio snaked through the crowd. Size was on their side, for the bodyguards were having a tough time moving their bulk in between the few cramped spaces unoccupied by the crowd. Finally the museum exit came into view. *Whew, we made it!* All three of them darted toward the doors at full speed.

Just as Veer and Jai felt the blistering hot air once again, they heard a muffled scream. To their horror, they glanced back to see an enormous hand covering Vidya's mouth as she screamed in agony. The same gigantic bodyguard with the piercing blue eyes was restraining her.

By instinct the brothers ran back inside to help her. Veer went straight for the bodyguard, lunging at him with a clenched right fist. The bodyguard had to use both of his hands and all of his massive weight to ward off the attack, which was just enough time for Jai to grab Vidya. The trio ran out the door before the bodyguard had a chance to grab Vidya once again.

Once they were outside, they continued to sprint, with Jai slowing down to keep pace with Veer and Vidya, until they reached the intersection between Twenty-first and O. Panting heavily, Vidya glanced back with her hawk-like vision to assess the situation.

"They're not following us anymore!" She sighed with relief.

"Yeah, but they'll find us soon enough," Jai interjected as his fingers flew over the buttons of his phone, rapidly punching in the numbers of his mousi's cell. "We'd better get out of the open like this. We're sitting ducks."

Vidya scanned the area for any large crowds that would provide good cover. "There! Across the street." Vidya was pointing toward an ice cream shop that was stuffed full of people who wanted to cool off from the hot sun. The trio walked briskly toward the store, constantly watching for the bodyguards until they were safely inside.

Within a few minutes, the trio saw Anu's battered old red station wagon pulling up at the intersection. They rushed inside, relieved to get as far away from the museum as possible.

"Why did you need to be picked up so quickly?" Anu looked at Vidya with frustration. "The traffic was so bad that by the time you called, I had just nearly reached home and had to turn back."

Vidya quickly glanced back at Jai, a questioning look in her eyes. Jai shook his head. She gulped in anticipation of what she was about to do, "Sorry Ma, but all off the tickets to museum were sold out. We couldn't get in." Vidya lied to her mother.

"I thought you said that the school gave them to you."

Thinking quickly on his feet, Veer butted in. "Sorry, Mousi, we had read it wrong. The tickets actually are only valid next weekend."

"You guys really need to be more careful."

Yes we do, Veer thought to himself. *Especially with one of the world's biggest corporations trying to capture us.*

Veer slowly stirred his drink with a straw, hearing the ice cubes clink together in his frosty refreshing glass of lemonade. He lay in his usual comfortable spot on the cozy sofa in Vidya's room where the trio was discussing the day's shocking events.

"All of Nanna's clues led us to the exhibit on the Gaffa virus," Jai started.

"Yeah, and it was somehow linked to the town that Dr. Juarez mentioned," Vidya said.

"And for some reason, Vaccine Corporation did not want us to find this out," Veer added.

"So what's our next move?" Jai asked. "There is nothing left in the Medley of Talents box, so I don't think that Nanna had any more clues for us."

There was a long pause as the trio racked their brains for ideas. "The only thing that I can think of," Veer broke the silence. "Is to physically go to Vaccine Corp. and dig for some more information."

"You mean you want to break into the organization that tried to kidnap us?" Vidya was in shock. "Veer, they were willing to abduct us in open daylight!"

"Veer is right," Jai said. "We've got no other option."

"Besides, Vidya, this is the only chance we've got to find Nanna."

Vidya looked long and hard into Veer's eyes. She finally spoke, "Fine, I'll admit it. I'm scared." She took a deep breath. Her voice had changed from its normal cheerful tone to that of pure fear. "When that man had grabbed hold of me, I seriously thought he was going to capture me and kill me. But we've got to find Uncle, even if it means risking our lives."

"All right, now that we've got that settled, how in the world are we going to break in?"

Veer, Jai, and Vidya sat in the comfortable seats of Jyothi's minivan, which sat motionless, stuck in the daily morning commute traffic jam.

"Aunty, thank you for taking me with you along with Jai and Veer for take-your-child-to-work day." Vidya disguised her fear with a cheerful tone.

Jyothi returned a warm smile. "Don't thank me, I'm just glad that you're excited to learn about what I do." Everyone in the car shuddered when a loud honk sounded from somewhere behind them, something people eventually got used to in the heavy DC traffic. "Unfortunately I'll be busy for most of the day because the deadline on our new project got moved up. But I don't think anyone will mind if you guys explore on your own a bit. Just be careful not to stray too far."

The van continued to inch along the highway until finally, a full hour later, it pulled up next to Vaccine Corp. headquarters. A large metal sign that was emblazoned with the Vaccine Corp. logo marked the entrance to the huge facility. As Jyothi rounded the corner, the trio was taken aback by the sheer massiveness of the complex. Enormous metal structures stood around a colossal concrete central building that seemed like it could house an entire city. The whole facility resembled a modern day castle, except the Vaccine Corp. fortress was at least ten times greater in size. As they neared the entrance, Veer started to feel a foreboding chill.

Once the electronic doors slid open to reveal the inside of the main building, they were immediately buffeted with a rush of cool air. With the most sensitive eyesight, Vidya was forced to squint as the bright fluorescent light reflected off white tiles. In fact, it seemed as if everything around them was pure white, a world without color.

Jyothi led them through the vast entrance area into a thin hallway at the other end. Surrounding them on both sides were large windows through which the trio could see virologists in white coats meticulously working in the lab. This hallway led to another, in which hundreds of test tubes and lab instruments lay neatly organized on shelves.

The hallway opened up into another vast space, this time filled with dozens of tiny cubicles, each one containing a computer monitor. A large sign that hung from the center of the workspace read "Technology."

After traveling through a maze of at least a dozen more cramped hallways, Jyothi finally paused in front of a door etched with her name.

"All right, here's my office." She paused to unlock the door. As she shuffled in her purse for keys, a man suddenly appeared behind her.

"Hey, Jyothi," he whispered into her ear. The man was middle-aged with receding brown hair revealing a strikingly large forehead. Jyothi shrieked in surprise. "I heard there was a dinner meeting at your place last month. How come I wasn't invited?"

"I'm sorry, Martin, it was a private executive meeting."

"All right, are you coming to the meeting today?"

"Yes, I just have to get these guys settled in," she said, finally opening up the door to her office. Before Martin could speak again, Jyothi quickly shuttled the trio inside and slipped in herself.

"Who is he?" Veer wondered.

"Just a coworker," she responded. "Listen, guys, I've got to run to this meeting upstairs." Just as she was about to exit, she paused for a moment. "Oh yeah, and I almost forgot. Could you guys take a look at that computer?" she said, pointing at a large dusty monitor in the back corner of her office. "It hasn't been working for over a year and the tech support crew here still hasn't gotten to it. With all that you learned from Samir, I'm sure you guys could figure it out."

"Sure thing, Amma," Jai responded.

Jyothi smiled as she left her office.

"All right we have to focus on getting this computer fixed for Amma, and then we can dig around for some more info about this Gaffa virus," Jai said.

Jai rolled his chair over to the desktop in the corner that was covered in clutter and Veer and Vidya followed. Together they popped open the side of the computer to reveal its internal workings. They scanned the complex wiring until Veer finally spotted the problem. One small wire was disconnected, seeming like only a tiny error, but it caused the whole computer to malfunction.

"That's strange," Veer said as he reinserted the wire. "How could this come undone just by itself? It has a pretty tight fit."

"It looks as if someone tampered with it," Jai responded.

The computer booted up surprisingly fast even though it was a fairly dated model. In a few seconds, a screen popped up with a single text field in the center that asked for a password.

"All right it's fixed. Now, how are we going to find out more about this whole Gaffa virus?" Veer said impatiently. "And how are we going to find information that will lead us to Nanna?"

"But it's not just like they are going to have files sitting around about him," Vidya said. "If they captured an innocent man, they probably have the information locked up somewhere."

Jai turned back toward the monitor. "Probably in the computer system."

"But how are we going to get the password?" Veer wondered.

The computer switched to its screen saver, a black screen with two lines in white font scrolling across the screen. It read,

"A leader, organizer, a Brooklyn man,
This is where your search began."

"That does not seem like something that would normally appear on a Vaccine Corp. computer desktop," Jai said. "The person who unplugged the wire must have set up the screen saver."

"Nanna must have done it," Veer replied definitively. "He probably wanted us to see whatever was on that computer."

"Let's not jump to conclusions, Veer," Jai said.

"It would make sense," Veer retorted. "Nanna led us here with all of the clues. And he could have easily taken Amma's office key from home. Once he broke into Vaccine Corp., he could have come here to this very computer."

"Assuming that's true, then I think that the screen saver might be a clue for the password," Vidya reasoned. "Do you guys have any ideas?"

"Let's think this through logically," Jai responded. "If the person who tampered with this computer was Nanna, then the search he is probably referring to is our search for him after he went missing. That search began with the clues he gave us in the Medley of Talents box."

"But look at the first line," Veer interjected. "He is referring to a person. A leader, an organizer . . ."

"Mr. Harrison!" Vidya exclaimed. "As the principal, he is the leader of our school. And he organized the Medley of Talents competition!"

"That's true, and there's no mistaking his New York accent. He must be from Brooklyn." Jai sounded excited.

"Let's give it a shot." Veer's fingers were already flying across the keyboard as he typed "Douglas Harrison" into the password text field.

"Welcome" appeared in large bold letters across the screen.

"Yes!" Vidya let out a cry of joy. "It worked!"

The computer loaded up the desktop. When it appeared only a single icon showed up on the center of the screen. Jai quickly double-clicked on it.

A picture immediately filled up the screen. The man shown was covered in huge red spots and his limbs and face were swollen beyond belief. He lay limp, sprawled across a hospital bed.

"Hey, that looks like the picture we saw in the museum," Veer exclaimed.

"Take a look at the date the picture was taken," Jai said, pointing at the bottom-left corner of the screen. "July 5, 2006. Isn't that when Nanna took that trip to India with Dr. Juarez?"

"Hey, click on the audio file," Veer said. Jai moved the cursor over to the top left and clicked on the audio icon.

"July 5, 2006." Samir's familiar deep voice emanated from the computer's speaker. "Dr. Juarez and I split up yesterday in order to be able to visit more places on behalf of Save the Smile to treat as many kids as possible. But when I reached this village Patnam, I could immediately sense something was terribly wrong. All of the streets were empty, and all of the houses were abandoned. It seemed like a ghost town. Then I started to hear a moaning sound, but it was especially hard to pick up because of my hearing problems. I followed the sound to the town hospital. When I poked my head through the hospital doors, I realized where everyone had been. Every square inch of the tiny facility was taken, sometimes as many as five people on the same bed. Where all the beds were taken, dozens of people lay on the floor, nearly on top of each other, groaning in pain.

"Then I was approached by a hunched over old man wearing a white coat. He asked me if I was the doctor from America. I nodded, and then he asked if I could help. I couldn't refuse. Then he told me that these were only the preliminary cases, and that the more advanced stages were in the tent out back. The entire town was infected, the worst disease I had ever witnessed.

"When the doctor pulled open the tent covers, I was speechless. The sight of those suffering people was permanently burned into my memory. It was the worst thing I have ever seen to this day."

The recording ended. Veer immediately clicked on the arrow at the bottom of the screen, eager to continue hearing of his nanna's discoveries. This time there was no picture, and only a single audio icon lay on the screen.

"July 6, 2006. Already, half of the town's population was wiped out by the sickness overnight." Samir paused for a moment. Fear and grief were evident in his voice. "I've never seen anything like it. Today I examined one of the few surviving victims of the disease. She was a young woman, in her early twenties. She was already in the later stages of the disease. Her entire body was covered in red lesions and her limbs were starting to swell. She seemed to be unconscious, but as I was conducting the examination, she suddenly awoke and started to scream in pain. I became so startled that I knocked over the test tubes and the shattered glass made a huge cut on my hands. She started to plead. 'Please help me,' she cried in broken English. I can still remember the look in her eyes. 'I have two children at home. Help me.' Then, before I could stop her, she grabbed my lacerated hands and continued to beg.

"It took me a second to realize what had happened. As I was administering morphine to her in order to reduce the pain, I had realized that her skin had come in contact with my cut!" Samir's voice was shaking. "I may have been infected."

The trio was horrified. "But he had to survive, we saw him afterward," Vidya whispered with fear.

"Let's just click on the next one and hear what happened," Jai responded.

"July 9, 2006. It is day three after the infection. I am still showing no symptoms of the disease. I do not want to sound optimistic, but I may not have contracted the sickness. Judging by the other cases, the virus infects and kills extremely quickly. If I had been affected, I would have been dead by now. In fact, I may be immune. Today I am going to draw some of my own blood to investigate. I wonder if this may help find an answer."

"July 11, 2006. Now, only a quarter of the town remains. The town's population is quickly dying off. I just don't know how to beat this bug."

"July 15, 2006. I travelled back to the US in hopes of contacting the Center for Disease Control to save what remains of the town. But it was too late, for by the time I reached here, I received word from the government back in India that the entire town was obliterated. Now I am working with the CDC to try to prevent further spread, yet they insist that nothing needs to be done because now the entire town is deceased and it was so secluded that no one else could make contact to transmit the disease. They did tests and assured me that I would not spread the deadly virus. I hope they are right, because if this bug spreads with its one hundred percent fatality rate, it may be the worst epidemic the world has ever seen."

"August 1, 2006. Today I analyzed some of the blood samples I took from the patients back in Patnam. When I put it under the microscope, what I saw shocked me. The virus was nothing like anything I have seen before. I just can't believe it mutated from a known virus. It just doesn't seem possible to change that many characteristics that fast. The only possible answer I can come up with is that this bug was manufactured. With the new technology I have just recently been researching, I realize that it is entirely possible for some sick, perverted unethical scientist somewhere," Samir was spitting the words from his mouth. "To have made this virus from scratch as part of some twisted experiment. I'm going to have to look into this."

"Do you really thing that this Gaffa virus was man-made?" Veer wondered.

"Maybe Nanna found out," Jai responded. "Let's keep on listening."

"August 15, 2006. Over the past couple of weeks, I've been looking into the idea that this virus was manufactured. And I started to think, if it was in fact a man-made virus, then it must have been deliberately placed there. So I just talked to a government contact back in India, who then relayed me to border security. I asked the commanding officer there if he noticed any suspicious men carrying any type of canister. He told me that he had, and the only reason that he let them through was because they were willing to pay him. What corruption! Letting those men through just for money could have very well led to the death of an entire town!" Veer had never heard Samir this upset and angry until now. "But I had to keep my calm when talking to him if I wanted to get the information I wanted. I asked him to describe these men to me. He recounted that there were three men, one old man flanked by a huge giant and a middle-aged brown-haired man. He also remembered that all three were well dressed, wearing suits and ties. They were too well dressed to be tourists. The last thing that he told me was that he noticed the words "Life's Ladder" on the canister. If I can find out what this means, I may be able to find the people that manufactured this virus."

"January 18, 2007. I've been doing some research lately into figuring out what exactly these two words, "Life's Ladder," refer to. Today I finally found the answer. Life's Ladder Incorporated is a small company that sells the parts necessary to build a machine capable of building viral DNA by itself. I called them up to find if anyone recently made any large purchases. They said that they mostly do business with universities as part of research. But just a year prior, for the first time a private company made a huge order of parts. But they wouldn't reveal the company's name for confidentiality." Samir let out a deep long sigh. "I had no choice but to break into their system. I just had to find out if these were the people who manufactured the virus. Life's Ladder had fairly good security, but I was still able to bypass it and access their database. It turns out that the company that was buying these products was none other than Vaccine Corp."

"Wow," Jai said, completely shocked. "I can't believe it. Vaccine Corp. manufactured the most dangerous virus the world has ever seen."

"*I* can't believe that Nanna hacked into a computer database," Veer responded. "I don't doubt his capabilities. I know he studied computer science in college and was practically a programming genius. But he would never use that knowledge to take advantage of others."

"I guess desperate times called for desperate measures," Vidya said. "Come on, there's more."

"April 21, 2007. I still can't believe that Vaccine Corp., the very place that Jyothi works, is the one responsible for manufacturing this virus. I've decided not to share this information with her in order not to jeopardize her career and our family. And I have no hard evidence to report to the police. The border security officer definitely won't admit to his corruption on record. If I try to point the police toward Vaccine Corp. with the leads I have, I will definitely get my wife fired. I've worked nonstop, day and night, over the past couple of months just trying to figure out what Vaccine Corp. was doing with this virus." Samir yawned, obviously sleep deprived. "Why would they just release it on one single town and wipe them out, then never use the virus again? The pieces just don't fit. I've tried everything in order to find out what they plan to do with the virus including trying to hack their database multiple times. But their security is just too tight. I can't break through from the outside. It seems as if the only option is to go through the inside. I'll have to physically go to

Vaccine Corp. and sniff around. But before I do, I'll have to do some research on the facility, to try and find where I can get this highly classified information about the virus."

"July 7, 2007. I have been preparing for the past couple of months to try to break into the Vaccine Corp. facility and figure out what they are going to do with this virus. I've done almost all of the research I needed to do and I know how to get into the Vaccine Corp. facility and where to find the information." Samir paused for a few seconds and a scratching noise was audible through the speakers. "But recently over the past couple of days, I've started to feel a bit under the weather and a strange rash has developed all over my ears. I've decided not to go until I'm completely better and ready for anything. Hopefully I can go soon, because time is of the utmost importance, for they can decide to use this virus anytime they want and kill millions of people."

"July 10, 2007." Samir was breathing extremely hard, panting into the recorder. "I've just come back from Vaccine Corp. headquarters. What I discovered there shocked me beyond belief." He paused for a moment to catch his breath. "Tonight I infiltrated the facility by taking Jyothi's security card to get into the building. But it only took me so far. After getting into the main building, I knew that I needed to get to Restricted Zone 17A, where the highest classified information is held. Only top-level executives can access this area. Jyothi did not have a high enough level security access to enter the zone, so I was stuck. But then suddenly I heard someone speaking through the door. I'm surprised I was able to hear anything at all!" Samir was referring to his hearing disability. "Somehow the voices were crystal clear even through the thick metal walls. Anyway, the most important and frightening part was the content of their conversation . . ." Samir gulped in anticipation of what he was about to reveal. "Vaccine Corp. is preparing huge quantities of the virus they released on Patnam, also known as the Gaffa virus. They plan to release this virus within the next three years," Samir paused again. "Worldwide. The entire human race could be in danger. Why would they do such a thing? For money of course. Since Vaccine Corp. also manufactured the cure for the disease, they are going to secretly disperse the virus and then tell everyone that they miraculously came up with a cure. Of course, everyone will pay lots of money for this cure that will save their lives, and Vaccine Corp. will come out the richest corporation on the planet. But for those who cannot access the cure in time, millions, if not billions of lives will be lost in the process. Vaccine Corp. must be stopped."

The trio was speechless. At any time, Vaccine Corp. could unleash this lethal Gaffa virus and wipe out humanity if they wished. And they were sitting in the headquarters of this evil corporation. Veer clicked on the next and very last audio file.

"September 4, 2007. Jai, Veer, and Vidya, if you are listening to this then you must have solved all of the clues that I laid out for you." Samir's tone was steely. "I'm sorry, it must have been pretty difficult, but I chose you three, and not Jyothi or Anu, because I knew you could do it in complete secrecy. I couldn't let anyone else know that I discovered Vaccine Corp.'s plan. Vaccine Corp. is incredibly powerful. The have bought off many police officers and they have ears everywhere. Even some of the highest-ranking politicians are their puppets. If word gets out that I figured out their plan, then all of our lives would be in danger. Also, notifying officials would at most delay

Vaccine Corp.'s time schedule. With the power they have bought, they could still accomplish their goal. Right now, I have to leave for a while to try to prevent Vaccine Corp. from unleashing the virus by any means possible." Samir paused for a moment. "But if you're listening to this, it probably also means that I have failed to stop them and I have been captured. Now I am passing this mission along to you. I know it is a lot to ask, but you guys have to destroy the virus in order to save millions of lives. Don't try to contact the police or the government, because if you do, Vaccine Corp. will immediately find you and stop you." Samir's tone suddenly changed. "But I want you to know that I am the proudest father and uncle in the world, and that you guys can stop them even if I couldn't. I'm sorry, but I have to go now."

After the recording was finished, not another word was said for over a minute. Veer, Jai, and Vidya were all deluged with the most intense emotions, ranging from disbelief to grief, rendering them incapable of doing anything. Finally after a full minute and a half, Jai was the first to speak.

"All right, it looks like it's up to us to stop this attack," he said. "I really hope Nanna is okay." Jai paused for a moment and for the first time since Samir disappeared, a single tear rolled down his cheek. But Jai quickly wiped it away and seemed more resolute than ever. "And we have got to stop Vaccine Corp. from spreading the virus."

Both Veer and Vidya stopped to wipe the streams of tears from their eyes. Veer sniffled and responded, "How are we going to do that?" Just then he spotted one more file left at the bottom left hand corner of the computer screen. "Hey, Jai, click on that last file." When it opened up, the trio saw an intricate picture of a large building with hundreds of measurements on the side of each line. At the top it read "Vaccine Corp HQ." "It looks like a blueprint of this complex."

As Vidya scanned the blueprint, ingraining every important detail into her near photographic memory, she suddenly noticed something. "Hey, guys, look at the bottom of the blueprint." In tiny font it read, "Remember, everything has its faults." "What's that supposed to mean?"

"No idea, but we have to focus on finding and destroying this virus right now," Jai said.

"All right, but where would they hide this virus or even keep information on the Gaffa virus project?" Veer wondered.

"The restricted zones!" All three of them realized at once, remembering Samir's audio file.

"Going into the restricted zones will be extremely dangerous," Vidya said. Both Veer and Jai just glared at her in response. "All right, all right. But how are we going to get in?"

"I don't know exactly. But our powers might come in handy!" Veer grinned.

The trio exited Jyothi's office and began to stroll along the hallways, acting as if they were simply exploring the facility. But all the while, Vidya was constantly scanning for something that would denote the location of the restricted zones.

"Vidya, did the blueprint say where the restricted zones were located?" Jai said.

"No, it didn't even refer to them once," Vidya said as they continued to search. After thirty minutes of combing through the labyrinth of hallways, the trio found nothing.

"This place is just too big," Veer said, frustrated. "We're never going to find anything."

"Just be patient, there's got to be a sign somewhere," Jai replied, though he was on the verge of frustration as well.

Vidya suddenly jumped in surprise. Strolling down the opposite hallway was Martin. "Isn't he supposed to be in a meeting?" she whispered as they ducked into a side hallway. "What is he doing here?"

"I don't know, but let's find out." Veer began to trail Martin.

"Veer, wait . . ." Jai tried to stop him but it was too late. Jai and Vidya had no chance except to follow.

The trio kept a considerable distance behind Martin, but Vidya constantly kept him in her line of sight. He was continuously glancing left and right, and Vidya could see beads of sweat erupting from his forehead from over fifty meters away. *He's obviously worried about something.*

Suddenly Martin stopped abruptly and glanced backward. If they had been a second slower, Martin would have caught the trio in plain sight. But Jai was too fast, pushing Veer and Vidya along with himself into the adjacent corridor in less than a split-second.

"That was too close," Jai whispered. "Veer, we've got to be more careful. We can't keep following him, we will get caught."

"But, Jai . . ."

"Actually, Jai, I think he's up to something," Vidya butted in. "Let's just trail him a little farther, we might get some useful information."

Reluctantly, Jai conceded and the trio cautiously moved toward the previous hallway. But when the trio returned, the corridor was empty! Vidya quickly scanned the hallway for any signs of Martin or where he could have gone.

"Got it!" Vidya exclaimed. She began to race down the corridor toward a doorway at the left, pointing at a small red sign posted above. When Veer and Jai caught up, they could finally see that the sign read Restricted Zone. Easily disguised, the door resembled any other except for the tiny sign and a nondescript electronic lock under the doorknob.

Veer tried turning the knob and it was obviously locked. "Guess there's only one way in." Veer gripped the door handle with two hands and twisted until his knuckles turned white. The metal creaked and groaned, bending under the immense pressure that Veer was applying.

"Stop!" Vidya whispered forcefully. "Someone's going to catch us because of all the noise that we're making. There's an easier way. I've got a better idea."

Vidya bent over to examine the lock underneath the now contorted door handle. She squinted her eyes, focusing hard on the black rubber number pads.

"Guys, remember these numbers," Vidya said after a few more seconds of intense examination of the keypad. "Two, four, six, and nine."

"Why? What are you doing?"

"I just figured out the numbers of the combination used to open the lock," Vidya said as she rapidly punched in numbers.

Both Jai and Veer quickly did the math in their heads. "That means only twenty-four possible combinations." Jai was first to answer.

"Exactly," Vidya responded. "And the only way we can get in is by trying all of them." After ten more different combinations, the light on the lock turned green and a quiet click followed.

Veer was completely puzzled. "How did you figure out which numbers were in the combination?"

"It was easy," Vidya replied. "I remembered reading somewhere that whenever human fingers contact another surface, they leave a residue of oil. All I had to do was use my magnified eyesight to see which numbers had the most residue in order to see which were pressed most often. Those were obviously the numbers that were used for the combination to open the lock." Both Veer and Jai were so amazed at how Vidya was able to cleverly utilize her powers that they paused for a moment, simply staring back at her in awe. "Come on, guys, we've finally got access to the restricted zone, let's have a look around."

Vidya turned the distorted doorknob. She slowly pushed the door open just enough for her head to fit through. Cautiously, she poked her head through.

"The coast is clear," she whispered.

Silently, Jai and Veer followed her inside the restricted zone. Once they entered, they suddenly felt a steep drop in temperature.

"It must be below freezing in here," Veer whispered through chattering teeth. Jai let out a deep breath, creating a white mist around his mouth.

They were on an elevated hallway bordering the entire room that was made entirely of metal. Dim red lights in the ceiling gave the room an eerie glow. The hallway surrounded a large central opening that went deeper underground. Across from them was a staircase that led to the central opening. But Martin was nowhere to be found.

"Where's Martin?" Veer wondered.

"We can't worry about him now. We can only focus on finding Nanna," Jai said calmly.

The trio crept stealthily along the side of the metal hallway to the staircase. Suddenly there was a loud thumping noise, and then a metallic clang. By instinct Jai darted to the nearest possible hiding place, bringing Veer and Vidya along with him. They listened for another sound but it did not come. Vidya quickly scanned the room, and no one was in sight.

Veer was the first down the stairs, slowly taking one calculated step at a time in order to not draw attention. Vidya followed and Jai brought up the rear. This floor was even chillier than the first, a sign that the trio was traveling deeper and deeper underground. The stairs led to a narrow hallway that took a sharp right angle turn. The trio stole noiselessly to the bend in the hallway and paused. They heard voices echoing from afar.

"Vidya, you've got to tell us how many people there are and where they are located," Jai whispered.

Vidya laid her back and hands flat against the wall and slowly turned her head around the bend. She was amazed at what she saw. The room was huge, at least over a football field in length. Large ten-foot tall vats covered the entire vast expanse with tight spaces in between just big enough to let someone through. Through these tiny spaces, Vidya saw the sources of the voices.

Two men in white coats were arguing about something, pointing at a computer monitor located in between them. Vidya did not even have to strain to see what was on the computer monitor located over three hundred feet away.

On the top, the title read "Samir Gupta" and underneath was one of the faces that Vidya had not seen for over a year and a half except in her mind's eye. In the picture, Samir was unconscious and his face was covered in huge bruises. Underneath, the page read "Status: Alive in holding cell 246. Due for execution in twenty-four hours."

The shock of Samir being alive, but also a day away from death was too much for Vidya to bear. Just as she was about to let out a scream of disbelief, she felt an immense pain in the back of her skull and her world went black.

CHAPTER 14

The first thing that Vidya felt when she awoke was an immense throbbing pain originating from the back of her neck and spreading throughout her entire upper body. She groaned in pain and turned over on her side to examine her surroundings. She was in a dimly lit room with the only light coming from flickering pale fluorescent lights. The room was composed of solely concrete, and a single toilet sat at the edge of the room. A small sign that read Room 215 was positioned above a metal door. From the corner in which she was nestled in, she could spot the outlines of Veer and Jai's bodies lying unconscious across the room. Then all of the memories started to come back. Recollections of Samir's discoveries flashed through her head. Then she remembered what had happened right before she was knocked out. *Uncle is still alive and we still have got to save him!*

Vidya sprung up off the rough floor and immediately ran over to wake Veer and Jai. She shook them both violently until finally they stirred. Veer moaned as he slowly rose from his uncomfortable concrete bed.

"Ughh," Veer winced in pain as he rubbed his neck. "What happened?"

"We let our guard down," Jai said disgustedly as he sat up. "That's what happened. And now look where we are. Stuck in a prison cell."

"Yeah and why didn't you warn us about the guards coming Jai? You brought up the rear," Veer responded angrily.

"Well, Mr. Big-Shot, you have super-strength, why didn't *you* fight them off?" Jai retorted.

"Stop it!" Vidya said with so much force that both Veer and Jai were surprised. "I didn't come all the way to Vaccine Corp., the most dangerous corporation in the world right now, and sneak into their restricted zones just to watch you guys bicker." Vidya's voice was gradually getting louder and her tone angrier. Then she took a deep breath and calmed down. "I came to find Uncle."

"But Nanna told us that he was probably dead and that we have to find the virus," Jai said after he had calmed down as well.

"Right before I was knocked out, I saw something on the computer. It said that Uncle was still alive and . . ." Vidya just couldn't say it after seeing Veer and Jai's reaction and their elated faces.

"And what," Veer said eagerly.

Vidya still could not tell them what she saw. "Vidya, we have as much of right to know what was on that computer as you do," Jai told her.

"I guess you're right," Vidya finally relented. She was fighting tears. "It said that he was going to be executed tomorrow."

Veer and Jai's expressions turned to complete dismay just as fast as they had become excited to find that Samir was alive. After deep thought, Jai spoke. "That means only one thing. We have got to find and save Nanna before they execute him."

"But how about the mission he gave us? He said that it was our priority to find and destroy this virus," Veer said.

"But we have no idea where this virus is and how to destroy it," Jai immediately responded. "And the only person who does and who we can trust is Nanna. In order to destroy the virus, we've got to get Nanna out first."

"But there is just one big problem," Vidya said as she wiped her eyes. "How about if he is already dead? There is no way of knowing how long we've been knocked out. Twenty-four hours could have already passed."

Suddenly there was a loud pounding noise against the door. "Hey keep it down in there." A gruff voice resonated through the walls. "Dr. Faize is coming in to see you."

The door swung open to reveal Dr. Faize, whom the trio quickly recognized from the museum. His old but chiseled and strong features emitted a sense of great power as soon as he stepped in the room. A man of his age would usually be stooped over a cane or in a wheelchair, yet he was surprisingly fit with an erect posture. His expensive-looking suit stretched over his toned muscles. He meticulously examined Veer, Jai, and Vidya with fiery blue eyes that had the passion and drive of a man thirty years younger. After a thorough inspection, Dr. Faize grinned widely, which revealed pearly white teeth. But his happiness was obviously not genuine.

"Jai Gupta, Veer Gupta, and Vidya Reddy." From Dr. Faize's tone, the trio felt like they were sitting in the principal's office. "Don't you know that it is rude to interfere with other people's business?" Dr. Faize started wagging his index finger mockingly. "Now why would you go sneaking around your mother's workplace?"

"How do you know our names?" Veer yelled back.

"Answer the question!" Dr. Faize was suddenly hot with anger.

"We were bored." Jai lied.

"Do you *really* expect me to believe that?" Dr. Faize glared long and hard into Jai's eyes and Jai was frozen in fear by the icy cold stare. "Now to answer your question, young Veer, we have been keeping an eye on you and your family for quite some time. I know all about you. And I also suspect that Samir Gupta, your father, sent you here to save him."

He's wrong, Nanna sent us here to destroy the virus. But better to act dumb and not blow the element of surprise. "Our father died over a year ago," Veer replied.

"Don't play stupid with me!" Unexpectedly, Dr. Faize raised his hand and slapped Veer forcefully across the face. Veer got up to retaliate, but Jai immediately put an arm out, barring Veer's way, and two burly guards ran in to protect Dr. Faize. Jai shot Veer the look that he always did when he wanted Veer to withhold his powers. "Feisty little one, huh," Dr. Faize said, eyeing Veer. "I know that Samir contacted you guys somehow in order to have you guys break him out of here. What a coward! Send your kids here to bust you out." Dr. Faize laughed derisively. "Only somebody like him would do that." Now Dr. Faize was trying to get a rise out of Veer, but Veer kept his calm. "Well too bad. You guys can't save your coward of a father now. It's too late. Samir is going to be executed within the next hour." Dr. Faize once again smiled widely, but this time the happiness, or sadism, was genuine. "And looks like you guys are stuck in a solid concrete cell with no way out." Dr. Faize gestured to the room around him. "Don't worry, you won't have to suffer in misery for too long. I'll have you three executed as well just as soon as my friend here, Mr. Avery," Dr. Faize pointed at an enormous guard who just entered the room. He had piercing blue eyes and an all too familiar scar running up his forearm. *He's the guard who attacked Jai!* "Coaxes the information out of you." Just as Dr. Faize was saying that, Avery was slowly sharpening a metal dagger. *Torture sounds more like it.* Veer gulped and looked over at Vidya and Jai. They too had similar expressions of utter fear. "But first we must oversee the execution of Samir Gupta." Dr. Faize continued to smile. With that, Dr. Faize, Avery, and the two other guards left the cell.

"It seems like we're done for," Veer muttered solemnly.

"Don't you see? This is good news," Vidya exclaimed. Both Veer and Jai just returned a blank stare. "Uncle hasn't been executed yet, we still have a chance to save him!"

"But how are we going to get out of this fully concrete cell?" Jai asked.

"Yeah, Vidya, we've got less than an hour to get out and find Nanna."

"I already know where he is, the computer said he was locked in room 246. Veer, can't you somehow bust through the door?" Vidya tried to keep them positive.

"I can try." Veer placed both of his hands on the side of the door and pushed with every ounce of his strength. The door did not budge at all. "There is no way this is an ordinary door. I should have easily opened it by now."

Vidya ran over to take a look. She peered in the tiny crack between the door and the concrete wall. Several thick steel bars ran through the crack, forming an unbreakable juncture between the door and the cell walls. "It seems as if they have got metal bars connecting the metal door to the concrete. They can probably only be unlocked from the outside."

"One way in and no way out," Veer said glumly.

"No, there has got to be a way out," Vidya responded stubbornly. She meticulously inspected the entire room, but the thick concrete covered everything, leaving not a single opening. Just as Vidya was about to give up as well, she spotted something. As she was using her near-microscopic vision to examine the walls, she found tiny hairline cracks webbing all through the concrete. "Everything has its faults," Vidya muttered, remembering what Samir told them.

"What?" Veer and Jai strained to hear Vidya.

"Everything has its faults!" Vidya repeated excitedly. "Remember the bottom of the blueprint?"

"Yeah, but what does it have to do with anything?" Jai asked.

"This wall is weakened by thousands of tiny faults in the concrete! That means---,"

"We could break through the cell walls!" Veer exclaimed, suddenly on the same track as Vidya.

"But even if we do, where would that take us?" Jai said. "What happens if we just end up in another cell?"

"Let me think." Vidya tried to picture the blueprint that she burned into her memory. "Well if we break either of these walls." She pointed to the sides adjacent to the door. "Jai is right, we will just end up in another cell. But if we break through that wall," this time she pointed at the wall opposite the door, "then we can get into the duct system that leads to all of the other cells."

"Just wondering, what does this duct system carry?" Veer interjected.

"I think the blueprint said something about sewage, but I'm not totally sure," Vidya responded. Veer felt nauseous at the thought of being in a sewer duct.

"I guess I'll do what it takes," Veer gagged. "It's time to take down that wall."

Veer charged wildly toward the wall with his right shoulder out in front like a battering ram. When he neared the wall, he tensed his muscles. But when his shoulder made contact, instead of the concrete shattering like Veer suspected, all of his energy was channeled back toward him. His joints smashed together painfully and Veer was thrown onto the ground.

Immediately Vidya ran over to help. Veer was slow to get up, rubbing his smarting shoulder.

"What happened? I thought you said the wall was weakened." Veer looked at the spot where he attempted to destroy the wall. The only evidence of his assault on the concrete was a small chip indented onto the wall.

"I guess it hasn't been weakened enough," Jai said.

"Well if I keep on hitting it in the same place, it might be enough to break through." Veer threw his fist at the wall with all of his might, but he was on the ground within seconds. The indentation on the wall now was only less than an inch deeper. "Third time is the charm," he said optimistically while rubbing his now swollen right shoulder. But after a third failed attempt to break through the wall, Vidya had enough.

"There is no way we are going to get through that wall in time. The only thing that you are accomplishing is hurting yourself." Vidya placed herself in between Veer and the wall to prevent him from trying again.

"But I think I can do it," Veer groaned through the pain persistently.

"Not without my help." Jai stepped in.

"What are you talking about, Jai?"

"What if you had a running start?" Jai immediately grabbed Veer by the shoulders and lined up at the opposite edge of the room. Jai planted his feet solidly on the ground in sprinters position behind Veer. Then he blasted off pumping his legs as quickly as he could while pushing Veer by the back. At the last second before they smashed into the wall, Jai let go and let Veer do the rest.

Veer redirected all of his momentum behind his fist and charged toward the wall. His speed from Jai pushing him towards the wall coupled with his enormous strength all behind a single booming punch was just too much for the weakening concrete. This time when Veer's fist contacted the wall, it crumbled to tiny pieces, submitting to the brothers' powers.

Veer dusted off his hands. "Now what?"

The sewage ducts smelled even worse than Veer expected. The trio was now crawling on their hands and knees through a stinky pool of brownish sewage glop. Every time one of them crawled forward, their hands pushing down on the sludge made a loud squelching noise. The only thing that made Veer force himself through the disgusting affair was what was at the end of the tunnel: his nanna.

Finally, after what seemed like ages of trudging through the putrid sewage ducts, Vidya cued them to stop.

"If I remember the blueprint correctly, Uncle's cell lies behind this wall," she said pointing to her right.

Once more, Jai and Veer combined their powers to annihilate the concrete cell wall. The trio quickly rushed in through the debris to greet the man they had searched for tirelessly since the day he had disappeared. Veer rehearsed this moment hundreds of times in his mind's eye while wishfully thinking that Samir was still alive, but now he still had no idea what he was going to say when he met his father again.

But when the trio entered the room, there was an eerie silence. The cell was empty.

"No! He has to be here!" Vidya cried.

"Are you sure that you remembered the blueprint correctly. What if you led us to the wrong room?" Veer said.

"But I'm positive that this is where they said they were holding Uncle." Tears were flowing down her face.

"No, Vidya is right." Jai was holding up a torn and faded photograph that he found on the cell floor. It was a picture of the entire family, including Vidya and Anu, that was taken at a picnic three years earlier. "Nanna was here."

"We didn't make it in time." Veer hung his head. "They've already taken him for execution."

CHAPTER 15

"**N**o!" Vidya wiped the tears from her eyes and her expression changed from grief to pure determination. "We haven't come this far just to give up. He might still be alive."

"But he's already been taken to be executed," Veer replied bleakly.

"Then we'd better hurry up before they actually do it." Vidya ran toward the door.

Both Veer and Jai also shook themselves out of their state of grief and followed her. The steel bars that bound the door to the concrete were unlocked, allowing Vidya to turn the doorknob and peek through.

"No one is in sight." All three of them slipped through the thick steel door.

They were in a wide spacious hallway lined with doors each posted with a cell number.

"Where are we going?" Both Veer and Jai turned toward Vidya.

"Why are you looking at me? The blueprint didn't say anything about an execution room. Why would it?"

"So we have no idea where we're going," Veer said.

The trio crept stealthily and speedily down the hallway, searching for a sign that might point them to the place that

Samir was being held. Once they reached the corner, Veer signaled that he would check for guards ahead. As soon as he turned his head to peek around the bend, a hand shot out and grabbed his neck.

"Ahhh, look who we have here." A tall brawny guard shoved Veer against the wall. "The three little kids have snuck out of their cell and gone out for a little stroll." Unexpectedly, the guard ruthlessly bashed Veer across the face. Both Jai and Vidya shuddered, frozen in shock. "Now that should teach you a lesson. Listen to me! Don't ever even think about. . ."

Suddenly, Veer clutched the guard's forearm and ripped it from his own neck. Then he whipped around and smashed the guard against the wall, pinning him with his left hand tightly gripping the guard's neck. In less than a second, their positions had reversed.

"No, you listen to me!" Veer was more forceful than Jai and Vidya had ever seen before. "You are going to tell us where Samir Gupta has been taken for execution and then never whisper a word of our little encounter."

The guard laughed. "Like I'll ever do that."

Veer wound up for a punch, drawing his fist back right in front of the guards face.

"No, Veer, don't do it!" Vidya tried to persuade him out of obliterating the guard's face. But it was too late, Veer already threw his fist with sickening speed and force directly toward the guard's head. Yet, at the last second, Veer directed his punch slightly to the right, missing the guard's head by a fraction of an inch. Now lying beside the guard's quivering head was a crater in the wall.

"Next time I won't miss." Now the guard was shaking uncontrollably with fear. Veer drew his arm back for another punch.

"Stop!" The guard finally consented. "I'll tell you where he is." He gulped. "Dr. Faize took him to the lab down at the end of the hallway." Then the guard smirked. "But you guys are already too late. By now the worthless coward's veins are probably shot full of poison."

Before the guard could speak another word, Veer slammed his fist straight under the guard's chin, knocking him out instantly.

"Never call my dad a coward." Veer let the guard's unconscious body fall limp on the floor.

"What did you do, Veer?" Vidya said fearfully.

"Don't worry, I held back," he responded.

Wasting no time, the trio sprinted down the hallway with Jai in the lead. As they travelled down the long vacant corridor, Veer could not help but think that there was something wrong. *This just seems too easy. There are no guards in sight. No one is trying to stop us.* Finally, after running a considerable distance, Jai stopped at a thick set of steel double doors.

"I guess this is it, the laboratory. Be ready to fight once we open these doors. They probably have this place heavily guarded," Jai whispered.

Veer smashed open the double doors, expecting to be confronted by at least a dozen guards. But all he found beyond the doors was a dark silent room. The trio entered cautiously, weary of even the tiniest noises and movements.

"There's nothing here," Vidya said as she utilized her ability to see even in the darkest of places.

Suddenly, bright fluorescent lights switched on, temporarily blinding them. A mechanical voice sounded from overhead.

"Initiating test sequence." Two small metal canisters dropped down from the ceiling. *What's happening?* Veer was starting to panic. "Commencing release of Gaffa virus in five seconds."

"It's a trap!" Jai gasped. "The guard led us to the virus testing chamber!"

Veer tried to open the doors, but they were secured shut. They heard a noise that sounded similar to air escaping from a bike tire. The metal canisters were releasing a vapor form of the virus. *Is this the end?*

"Subjects will experience symptoms in thirty seconds."

Veer started to count up to thirty seconds in his head. Veer tried to block the images of the victims of the Gaffa virus from his mind, but it was impossible. *Ten seconds.* The horrible red painful lesions and the huge inflammation, the seizures, paralysis, the thought of it all was just too much to bear. *Twenty.* Then after all of the suffering came death. Veer did not know what to think of it other than that he did not want to die with the feeling of failure, knowing that he was never able to save Samir. *Thirty.*

Veer was expecting excruciating pain, but it did not come. In fact, he could not feel any of the symptoms at all.

"What's happening?" he asked Jai.

"Nothing," Jai responded. "And now I know why. It all makes sense now."

"What are you talking about?" Vidya inquired. "Why aren't we all suffering from the virus right now?"

"Don't you remember Nanna's audio recording? He said that a strange rash had developed all over his ears."

"Yeah, but what does that have to do with anything?" Veer still was not clear on what Jai was getting at.

"We all had strange rashes that suddenly developed also. Then a couple of days after the rash . . ."

"We developed our powers," Vidya interjected, starting to realize Jai's discovery. "And a couple of days after Nanna had the rash, when he invaded Vaccine Corp., he was suddenly able to hear properly again."

"Not just properly, he was able to hear well, incredibly well. Much better than the average human," Jai said. "Before the rash, I started off slow. Vidya started off nearly blind and Veer was extremely weak. But afterward, I became the fastest kid in the school, Veer the strongest, and Vidya had amazing vision."

"Our greatest weakness became our greatest strength," Veer mumbled. "But still, what does this have to do with the Gaffa virus?"

"Well, remember how Nanna was exposed to the virus back in Patnam. He thought he didn't contract the disease because he was immune, but I don't think he was," Jai responded. "I think the virus mutated inside him."

"The museum did say that the Gaffa virus had a high mutation rate," Vidya agreed. "Maybe the virus changed from attacking everyone's weaknesses to turning their weakness into a strength."

"It's a good virus." Veer finally understood. "And when Nanna got back from Patnam, he gave it to us, the people which he was in most contact with."

"But why didn't Amma or Mousi get the virus also?" Jai wondered.

"Well, the mutated virus could possibly harbor in only certain people, and that's why Nanna didn't give the virus to everyone he met," Veer responded. Then he shook himself out of the awe of their recent discovery and the shock of their near-death experience and focused on the task at hand. "What are we doing here discussing the particulars of this virus? We've got to go and save Nanna!"

"But we still don't know where the lab is." Jai was hopeless.

"We don't need to," Vidya responded. "They are going to have to check on us after the testing is completed. We just have to wait until they send a guard, hide while he checks on us, and then follow him back to the lab."

"Where do we hide?" Veer wondered.

"Leave that up to me," she responded.

Vidya spotted the guard walking briskly toward them through the small window on the door to the testing room. He was speaking into his walkie-talkie, reporting every detail of his surroundings.

After the guard was about fifty feet away, Vidya whispered, "Now!" Veer grabbed the light switch and pulled down as hard as he could. The metal switch creaked and groaned, and finally bent under the immense force. Now the switch was jammed in the Off position, shrouding the room in darkness. The trio then went and hid in the far corner of the room.

Vidya could see the guard cautiously approaching the testing room door, but she was completely invisible to him in the darkness. The guard slowly turned the handle of the door and entered the room. He headed toward the light switch on the side wall, poking and prodding everything in his path in an attempt to locate the perpetrators. When he reached the switch, he tried in vain to turn it on and grunted with effort as he pushed on the jammed piece of metal.

As the guard struggled with the switch, Vidya cued Jai. Upon hearing Vidya's voice, the guard's hand immediately clutched the holster of his gun, so he was ready to draw at a moment's notice. But before the guard could locate the trio, Jai blew by him and dashed toward the door. The door already had swung open before he even had a chance to catch a glance of Jai.

Reacting quickly, he sprinted out of the testing room to try to capture Jai. But Jai was too quick for him. Jai darted back into the room before the guard could blink his eye.

From her vantage point back in the testing room, Vidya could see a frustrated expression cross the guard's face. It remained there only for a split second, but it was enough for Vidya to know that he had fallen for their bait. He turned back and started to sprint down the hallway, searching for Jai. *And when he doesn't find Jai, he'll go straight to his boss, Dr. Faize. He will lead us straight to the lab.* Vidya was satisfied that her plan had worked, but still incredibly worried that they would not make it in time. And by the looks on Veer and Jai's faces, she could tell they felt exactly the same.

The trio followed the guard while ignoring their growing anxiety that made their stomachs churn. They followed the guard just as they had followed Martin, keeping a safe distance and ducking at even the slightest turn of his head. Unfortunately, the guard was much more aware than Martin and he constantly swiveled his head left and right trying to find the trio, forcing Jai to push the other two aside every couple of seconds.

Finally the guard turned the corner of one of the many interconnecting hallways and paused in front of two large double doors. He disappeared beyond the doors for a few seconds, then returned with another security guard. In order to stay hidden from the guards' view, the trio stayed behind the corner of the intersecting halls. They were too far away to hear what the guards were discussing, but Vidya tried to lip-read from a distance.

The two guards were conversing heatedly. The guard who tried to capture them explained that one of them escaped from the testing room. The other guard, his superior from what Vidya could make out, disciplined him harshly for his failure. The first guard responded by recommending that they send multiple guards to fan out and search for the fugitive. But his superior simply shook his head. He said that he was under direct orders from Dr. Faize to remain in front of the lab until the execution was finished. Vidya thought she saw the superior guard saying something about Dr. Faize being paranoid, but she could not be sure.

"All right, Dr. Faize isn't taking our bait. Instead of sending the guards to look for us, he is keeping them right in front of the lab," Vidya whispered to Jai and Veer. "We're going to have to find a way around them."

"Around them?" Jai and Veer looked at each other quizzically. "Sorry, but the only way is through them," Veer responded.

"Through them!" Vidya was shocked. "They probably have a whole army of guards waiting for you in there. There is no way you can fight all of them!"

"Come on, Vidya, we don't have time to find a way around them. Nanna is on the verge of death. We've got to go in and save him," Jai said. "And Veer and I think we can take them. All of them."

Before Vidya could retort, both Veer and Jai charged toward the double doors. Veer and Jai knew that Vidya was right as soon as the doors swung open. Over a dozen guards stood blocking the entrance of the lab. Each of them stood over six and a half feet tall, with every inch of their body covered with bulging muscles. They were the biggest men that Veer, Jai, or Vidya had ever seen. *They look like NFL linebackers in suits,* Vidya thought to herself.

"What are you doing outside of your cells?" The front guard addressed them. "Johnston, will you please escort these kids back to their holding cells." Agitation was clear in his voice.

The smallest of the guards, who was still huge by any other standards, stepped forward and smiled wickedly. "Of course." He walked casually toward Jai and Veer, not expecting a fight from either of them. Suddenly, Veer ran up to Johnston and threw a huge punch straight at the guard's forehead. Immediately, he dropped to the ground, unconscious.

Then the fight began. Half of the guards stampeded forward at both Veer and Jai causing the ground to tremble. Veer assumed a powerful stance and held his ground while Jai ran straight at the attackers.

The foremost guard lunged straight at Jai, fully extending his body in order to try to tackle him. But Jai nimbly sidestepped out of the way, causing the guard to fall flat on his face. The next three guards came toward him at all sides, throwing powerful punches and kicks. Jai bobbed and weaved, speedily evading all of the blows. He then started to retaliate with well-aimed punches at the guards' weak points. Yet no matter how many times he hit them, his punches just did not seem to have an effect on the brawny guards.

On the other hand, Veer's punches were much more effective. He took enormous swings at the guards, crushing whatever his fists came into contact with. Veer brawled his way through the first three guards with his fists shooting out like pistons. When the fourth guard stepped toward him, Veer threw an uppercut straight into his chin, knocking him senseless. But as soon as Veer was finished with the first four guards, five more stepped forward to take their place.

Jai's punches simply were not wearing the guards down. As he continuously dodged the guards' attacks, an idea struck him. *If the virus made me incredibly fast, then it must have strengthened my leg muscles.* He ducked under an incoming punch. *That means instead of punching, I should kick!* Jai avoided three attacks simultaneously, and then he lifted his foot to prepare for a roundhouse kick. Jai swiveled his hips and extended his leg, smashing his foot directly into one of the guard's stomach. The guard immediately fell to the floor. *That's it!*

This time when the guards charged at Veer, they anticipated his punches and evaded all of them easily. Then four of the guards grabbed each of his limbs and pinned him painfully to the floor. Before Veer could even react, the fifth guard came crashing down upon him. The guard raised his fist then brought it down ruthlessly upon Veer's head. Veer cried out in pain. Then the guard did it again. And again. Each time the guard hit Veer, the pain dulled out all of his thoughts and brought him closer and closer to unconsciousness.

Jai was completely unaware of Veer's situation across the room. He had enough to deal with himself. The other two guards started to close in on him, but Jai lashed out with two more powerful kicks. Then even more guards started to barrage him with more blows. There were just too many fists for Jai to avoid, and he was starting to succumb to the guards' attacks. Jai had no other choice but to retreat toward the wall.

Veer was hanging on to the last edge of consciousness he had left in him. But as the guard continued beating down upon him, he was starting to let go and give up. He could not believe that he had gotten this close to finding Samir, but had failed. He did not want to go out this way.

"Veer, Jai, Vidya!" He dreamt that he heard Samir calling him. "Veer, Jai, Vidya!" It was louder this time. Was he dreaming? It took a second for Veer to realize that the voice was real!

The thought of his nanna being in hearing distance from him galvanized Veer. He was not going to take this thrashing any longer. Veer drew every ounce of strength he had left in him into raising his right arm from the guard's clutches. But the guard was not going to let go easily. Veer struggled, pushing with all of his effort. Finally, Veer lifted his arm from the ground, and brought the guard with it. The guard was surprised that this scrawny teenager was lifting his bulky frame off the ground, but he still did not let go. Veer ignored the burning pain in his arm and continued to force his arm into the air. When his arm reached its peak, he swung it along with the attached guard into the other guard pinning his left arm. The enormous collision between the two guards knocked them both unconscious and released both of his arms. With both of his hands free, Veer smashed both of his fists into the guards holding down his legs. Now all that was left was to get revenge on the fifth guard who ruthlessly beat his face.

Jai was trapped. Four guards were edging closer and closer to him by the wall, ready to pounce at any second. For fun, one of the guards threw a cheap shot right into Jai's gut. Jai doubled over and started to gag, but soon swallowed the pain. He needed to think, fast. *Is there any way out of here? I can't go through them or under them. They'll just stop me in my tracks.* The same guard lashed out another blow at Jai's head. The pain was starting to become intolerable. *So the only way is over them.* The guards were preparing themselves to attack, readying to tackle Jai and smother him. The guards were leaping through the air toward him, but at the last moment Jai sprinted straight at the wall.

Veer got up and stretched his sore arms casually, knowing that the fifth guard was no match for him one on one. Nevertheless, this guard was still the biggest and strongest-looking of all the guards he had fought so far. The guard smiled and held up two fists, both covered in Veer's own blood. He was not going to back down. Veer ran straight at the guard, getting skimmed by the guard's quick punches. When he came into striking range, Veer wound up and smashed his fist straight at the guard's chest. His punch sent the guard flying straight into the wall behind and knocked him out in less than a second.

Jai was on a direct collision course with the wall in front of him. But just as he was about to crash, he pushed off the ground and set his foot onto the wall. This transferred all of his momentum from horizontal to vertical, allowing him to speed upward toward the ceiling. Jai could not believe that this was actually working. But of course the momentum did not last, forcing Jai to jump off the wall after taking a couple of steps. While in midair, Jai did a somersault over the guards. He then landed on the opposite side facing them and had successfully escaped from their clutches. Jai utilized the split-second that the guards were distracted with disbelief to take the offensive. He dealt out four menacing kicks that knocked them out instantly.

Bruised, sweating, and panting, Veer and Jai looked at each other from across the room. They had made it through in one piece, though Veer's face was now a bloody mess and Jai could feel a couple of cracked ribs.

"How many did you take out?" Veer asked his brother.

"I think I counted nine."

"Hah! Beat you by one!"

"Did not. Johnston doesn't count. He wasn't even a fight."

But as the two brothers walked toward the laboratory door, they realized that this was not the time for joshing around. They heard suppressed screams of pain coming from inside. *Nanna had the highest tolerance of pain out of anybody I've ever met,* Jai thought to himself. *I've never heard him complain once about anything hurting. They must be doing something horrible to him in there.*

Jai and Veer anxiously rushed toward the lab entrance, knowing that time was running out. They needed to get Samir out of there fast. Veer busted open the lab doors and they charged inside. But before they could take more than two steps into the lab, they were stopped in their tracks by the biggest guard by far. Avery, the seven-and-a-half-foot tall colossus, stood blocking their path.

Vidya watched the fight unfold while staying hidden in the corner. *Can I help in any way?* she thought to herself as she watched both Veer and Jai obliterate half of the guards. *But they're doing fine right now and I'll just get in the way. Veer's strong and Jai is fast, which are both qualities that help in a fight. All I can do is see things. How would I help?*

But then Vidya stared in agony as she saw the fight suddenly turn when Jai was trapped in the corner and Veer was getting beaten into a pulp by five guards. She started to run over to help, but then stopped herself. *I'll just get caught by one of the guards, and then they can use me as leverage. That would just make things worse.* She bit her nails nervously as Veer and Jai were edging closer and closer to defeat. She felt horrible because she knew she could not do anything about it. But finally, things turned around once more, and the brothers fought their way past the final guards.

Vidya was relieved once the fight was over and ran over to join them. But before she could even make it down to the end of the hall, Veer and Jai already barged into the lab. Thinking that they had eliminated all of the possible security that could have guarded the lab, Vidya was shocked to find Avery waiting for the brothers. *They should have waited for me before going in blindly, I could have warned them!* Then she started to calm herself down. *They just defeated nineteen guards, how could one be any problem?*

Veer wound up and threw an enormous punch at Avery's stomach, which was at Veer's chest height. But Avery fluidly stepped out of the way and used his arms to redirect all of Veer's power against him. Veer ended up smashing his head against the wall and slumped to the ground, stunned temporarily.

Avery's laugh sounded like a lion's roar. "I've learned a couple of tricks since the last time we've fought. It's called Tai Chi."

Vidya could tell that Jai was angry. He stepped in and charged straight at Avery. Jai threw a barrage of quick yet powerful and well-aimed kicks at the monstrous guard, but Avery's reflexes were just too fast. He blocked every single one of Jai's kicks with his muscular forearms that easily absorbed the blows. To Vidya, it looked like Avery was just doing a practice sparring. Once Avery had enough, he shot out his hand and grabbed Jai's neck.

"Déjà vu, huh?" Avery said as he slowly strengthened his clutch around Jai's neck, crushing his windpipe. "Except this time, no little brother to save you." Avery brutally threw Jai to the floor.

Vidya had to help quickly. If she did not do anything, Veer and Jai would be seriously injured or worse. Her heart started to race and her hands grew cold just at the thought of it. Thinking quickly, she ran over to one of the unconscious guards and searched his suit. Finally, she found the object she was looking for. It was cold to her grip and surprisingly heavy, as if it was made of lead. When she pulled it out and held it in her hand, it looked like it just did not belong there. A wave of negative emotion flooded through her. She felt anxiety, anger, and grief all tumbling through her. But she had to do what she had to do in order to save her closest friends.

Just as Vidya was about to point the gun at Avery's chest, she saw Veer and Jai slowly recovering. There was still hope! She glanced around the room, trying to formulate a plan. One came quickly, and she was incredibly glad that it was one that involved no bloodshed.

Avery noticed the brothers rising from the ground. Before he could act, Vidya aimed and fired. What followed was a huge foamy explosion. Afterward, water started to pour down from the ceiling and a siren sounded. Fragments of a fire extinguisher lay littered on the edge of the room. Vidya was glad she had not missed.

Vidya's diversion distracted Avery for less than a second. But both Jai and Veer took advantage of Avery's confusion. Jai kicked hard at the guard's ankles, causing him to lose his balance. Veer dealt the finishing blow, a sharp punch at the back of the neck. With that, the big guard finally toppled to the floor.

Now that Avery had fallen, Vidya rushed over. She hugged them both tightly, tears of both happiness and relief coming from her eyes.

"Ow, that hurts, Vidya." Jai felt his broken ribs. "But thanks, we definitely could not have done it without you."

Veer interrupted their conversation. "Hate to break up the celebration, but we're still not done, guys. Nanna is still in trouble!"

They followed the shouts of pain further into the huge lab. From the entrance, they could not spot Samir, meaning that he had to be located somewhere in the back that was concealed with walls covered in the Vaccine Corp. logo. Lavender tiles gave the room a false sense of comfort, yet with each step Vidya took, more goose bumps spread over her skin. To her left stood large vats of a viscous clear liquid that bubbled incessantly. She wanted to take a closer look, but there was just no time.

The screams of agony gradually grew louder, meaning that they were finally closing in on Samir. Once they reached the rear wall, the shouting suddenly stopped. All three of their hearts skipped a beat. *Is that it?*

CHAPTER 16

Fear coursed through their veins. As an immediate reaction, Veer busted through the door that led to the back of the lab and Jai sprinted through. But as soon as he entered the back of the lab, Jai was frozen into place in shock.

An emaciated man with a scraggly graying beard lay upon a hospital bed, sweating uncontrollably. Beside was a grinning Martin, who was obviously enjoying administering the torture. And on the opposite side sat the leader of Vaccine Corp. himself, Dr. Faize.

At first, Jai did not even recognize the man, thinking that he had found the wrong person. But when he looked into the man's eyes, Jai knew it was his father. Yet it seemed as if he was looking at a ghost of his father lying in front of him. Samir was purely skin and bones. His face was gaunt, making him look decades older. His long dirty hair and beard masked his features, and his formerly large frame was shrunken to a meek skeleton. To anyone else, Samir was a completely different man.

Jai could see the words forming in Samir's mouth. "You came."

"Look who joined the party," Dr. Faize said calmly. "Now just how did you get past my security?" Somehow he did not seem surprised at all.

None of them answered.

"Not going to talk, all right, then we'll just have to take care of this affair." Dr. Faize was peering into a syringe filled with a dull greenish liquid. He flicked the syringe in order to remove all of the bubbles, preparing to inject. "You see, all of this time we were about to give your father a lethal injection to execute him once and for all. But then he said something about the Gaffa virus undergoing a critical mutation, and it sparked my curiosity. So I had Martin here try to *convince* your father to tell us more."

Martin was still grinning widely. Beside him was a pile of empty syringes that had residues of another bluish substance inside. "I gave him a toxin that affects the body's nerve cells. It gives the sensation of excruciating pain throughout the entire body. Too bad I can't give him any more. One more injection and it'll push the body over its limit causing shock."

"But you three came right in time, I'm sure even the tiniest scratch on one of you will get him to squeal." Dr. Faize laughed, and then nodded at Martin. Martin pulled out a knife that he was concealing under his white jacket and started walking toward the trio with his smug grin still plastered across his face.

The expression of fear shot through Samir's eyes. As Martin edged closer, Veer charged right at him. Martin was taken aback and held the knife in front of him in self-defense. Veer easily knocked it aside and smashed his fist straight into Martin's big forehead. Martin crashed to the floor, not even giving a fight.

Dr. Faize started to applaud, which was the complete opposite reaction from what Veer expected. "Bravo, well done." He continued to clap. "You took the bait and confirmed my suspicions." His face once again showed genuine happiness.

"What are you talking about?" Veer was taken aback.

"You mean you don't know already?" Dr. Faize continued to smile. "I thought you guys were smart. Didn't you even win the Medley of Talents competition?"

"How do you know about that?" Jai was beginning to get worried.

"Oh, you think that by destroying a couple of our microrecorders, you could get me off your backs? I had agents watching you twenty-four-seven." Dr. Faize's anger flared. "I knew that something fishy was going on, but you three just refused to use your powers. But now, after that magnificent display of strength, I could finally put things together. Now I know how a pitiful weakling could get so strong." Then Dr. Faize turned toward Samir. "It was all thanks to you, Samir. Once we caught you sneaking around our labs, we couldn't release you, could we? You saw too much. During this past year, I tried again and again to *convince* you to tell us what you knew about our plan so that we could cover our tracks. But you just wouldn't say a word. But I just had to do a little research on you to find out about your trip to Patnam on the Save the Smile effort. What a noble man." Dr. Faize feigned admiration. "That's how you found out about our plan and tried to stop us. How naive!" He laughed. "You really think that you could take us down?" He wiped tears of laughter from his eyes. "But now I know that you contracted the virus in Patnam. Then it changed inside of you and you gave it to him." Dr. Faize pointed at Veer. "Really, Samir, I sincerely thank you from the bottom of my heart for telling me about this mutation," he said sarcastically. "Now all I need is to do some more testing on this performance-enhancing virus."

"Why?" Jai asked him.

"Wow, you really are slow. So I can manufacture and sell it, obviously. A virus that transforms weaknesses into strengths would be Vaccine Corp.'s most lucrative product to date," Dr. Faize responded. "If you would please come with me, Veer," he beckoned.

"Why would I just hand myself over to you?"

"Because if you don't, your father dies," Dr. Faize responded calmly as he placed the syringe filled with green liquid on the surface of Samir's skin.

"Don't do it, Veer!" Samir said with as much force as he could muster.

"Please stay quiet." Dr. Faize slapped Samir cruelly across the face and started to poke the syringe into his skin. "Veer, you wouldn't want your father's death on your conscience after coming all of this way to save him, would you?" Veer started inching toward Dr. Faize.

Vidya was at a loss of what to do, frozen into place with fear. *If Veer stays, Uncle dies. But if he goes, then he'll be tested on like a lab rat. And after they are finished they will probably kill him anyway.* It was impossible for her to choose between equally horrible options. She looked over at Jai to see if he could do anything. But just like her, he was stuck in place. Tears started to well up in her eyes. *No, I can do something about this.* She shook herself out of it. Immediately, her eyes were drawn to the pistol that she still had clenched in her hands. Trembling, Vidya slowly lifted the gun and pointed it squarely between Dr. Faize's eyes.

Dr. Faize was still intently focused on Veer and it took him a moment to realize that a gun was being pointed at him. But once again, Dr. Faize's reaction was completely opposite from the expected. This time, he laughed heartily. "You wouldn't dare kill me. From all of this time I have been watching you, the one thing that I gathered is that you wouldn't even harm a fly."

She was about to reply with a bitter remark, but she held herself back. *He's right. I could never murder anyone even if Uncle's and Veer's life hung in the balance.* Vidya sadly admitted as she lowered the gun. *But I can't just watch him kill Veer or Uncle in cold blood.*

"That's what I thought," Dr. Faize said coldly. "Too weak."

She watched helplessly as Veer walked toward Dr. Faize, who still pressed the needle close to Samir's neck. Just as Veer was about to hand himself over, an idea formulated in Vidya's head. It was extremely risky, for if she missed ever so slightly then she could end up seriously injuring, or even killing Samir. But it had to be done, or else either Veer or Samir would be sent to their grave.

Vidya forced herself to stop shaking and hoisted the gun once more. Dr. Faize was slightly surprised.

"If you shoot me, half a milliliter of poison will be injected into his veins. It will kill him. Painfully and slowly."

Vidya stared at her tiny target, the syringe itself. Less than an inch to her left, and the bullet would hit Samir's neck. She had to be perfect.

Vidya felt her heart pounding rapidly in her chest and could almost envision the adrenaline coursing through her veins. She was beyond nervous. Vidya used her improved vision to align the barrel of the gun directly with the glass syringe. Then she pulled the trigger.

Vidya closed her eyes and prayed that the bullet would not hit Samir. She prayed that they all make it out of this alive. She prayed that they could all be happy once again.

The sound of shattering glass was the answer to her prayers. Vidya opened her eyes to find broken shards lying on the floor in a pool of the greenish liquid. The bullet had met its mark, and she had succeeded.

Everyone was so surprised at Vidya's course of action that they were frozen into place temporarily. Then the mayhem broke loose. With the syringe no longer poised at his neck, Samir tried to wriggle free of his bonds and Jai ran over to help. Meanwhile, Dr. Faize grabbed his laptop and started to type in commands in a frenzy. In response, Veer ran up to the leader of Vaccine Corp. and punched him directly in the jaw.

Veer made sure that the blow was not strong enough to knock out Dr. Faize instantly because he wanted the evil man to feel pain for all that he had done. But Dr. Faize just seized the opportunity to follow through with his plans on the laptop. Fighting to stay conscious, Dr. Faize typed in the last couple of commands.

"Now the world will be introduced to the Gaffa virus," Dr. Faize said smiling, with blood dribbling down his chin. With one final heave, Dr. Faize pressed the enter button on the laptop then faded out of consciousness.

A siren started to sound and the entire left half of the laboratory sprung to life. Huge machines raised up from below the tiles next to the vats of the clear liquid and large tubes dropped down from the ceiling. The machines were comprised of a single enormous robotic arm mounted on top of a container filled with small canisters similar to the ones that were in the testing room. Simultaneously, all of the robotic arms bent down and clutched the canisters. They then dipped the canisters into the vat of clear liquid and filled them to the brim with the viscous substance. Lastly, the machines sealed the canisters and placed them under the tubes overhead. The tubes sucked up the canisters and sent them off in an instant. Then the process was repeated.

"What's happening?" Veer shouted over the sirens.

Samir freed himself from the last of his bonds and leaped up from the stretcher with surprising agility. But once he was on his feet, the sound of the sirens weakened him because of his super-sensitive hearing. He began to fall to the floor, but Veer and Jai quickly ran over to help him up.

Samir cupped his hands over his ears. "Faize just initiated the emergency release sequence," he yelled. "Right now, Vaccine Corp. is preparing to release the virus worldwide. From what I remember seeing when I hacked into the system, the virus will be packed into canisters and transported in an armored truck to a central shipping location. From there, it will be sent to dispersal points on all five populated continents. We have to destroy the virus and whichever canisters that have already been packed to be sent. If we don't, I just don't know what will happen." Then Samir paused for a second and the tone of his voice dramatically changed from pure determination to tenderness. "I know we don't have the time, but I just want to say that I am more proud of you three than a man could possibly be. Thank you for coming, I know it took an amazing amount of courage and strength. But that is why I chose you, because I knew you had it in you. I don't even know how you got all the way here, Veer couldn't have possibly just bust through everything with that awesome strength, could he?"

Veer laughed. "No, Nanna, we had a couple of other tricks up our sleeves. Vidya now has powerful vision that she used to get us through security, while Jai and his speed helped me take down the guards. It was a team effort."

Samir had a look of bewilderment. "All three of you got the virus!" But then he shook himself out of it. "We can talk after we are done. Now that we have all these resources," he said pointing at the trio. "Taking down the Gaffa virus won't be impossible."

Samir improvised an entire plan to take out the virus. Just as he was about to finish explaining the final details, his ears twitched and a look of utter fear crossed his face.

He mouthed a single word, "Jyothi." Not wasting any time Samir started to race over to the lab exit. "Vidya, come with me," he yelled, and then turned toward his sons. "Jyothi is in trouble, but Vidya and I will take care of it. You two have to destroy this virus alone. Just follow the plan. I know you can do it."

Jai caught up to Samir in less than a second. "Wait, how will we know where to find you?"

Samir looked down at his filth-covered body all the way to his grime caked feet. "Don't worry, I'll leave a trail for you to follow." With that, he and Vidya left the lab as the siren continued to sound.

The brothers knew that time was of the utmost essence and immediately began to carry out Samir's plan. Veer smashed a hole into the lab wall for Jai to sprint through in order to follow the vacuum ducts. It was Jai's job to track down the canisters that were already being sent off to be shipped away. Meanwhile, Veer had to take care of dismantling the huge machines that continued to pack and seal the virus.

Veer attacked the closest machine with an onslaught of punches. He created deep dents in the metal covering of the robotic arm, but it continued to function flawlessly. Veer persisted and continued to maul the machine until it finally ground to a stop.

Veer looked at the battered machine while panting heavily and sweating profusely. He knew that he was taking way too long to destroy one single machine, for at least a dozen more lay ahead of him. Not only was his method inefficient, but also Veer's body could not hold up much longer, especially after the battle with the guards. There had to be another way.

Jai sped down the dark innards of Vaccine Corp., following the vacuum tubes overhead. He raced down at a sickening speed, fast even for his pace. But ahead was even more darkness waiting for him. As more and more time passed, Jai was beginning to get worried. The tunnel seemed unending and his legs felt like they could give way any moment. He was beginning to pant as his lungs worked hard, a feeling that Jai barely ever experienced since getting the virus. Was he lost?

Vidya was shocked at how quickly and easily Samir moved even after losing most of his strength. She struggled to keep up with him as he followed the sound of Jyothi's voice. He knew exactly in which hallways to turn and where to look out for guards. It seemed as if a map of every nook and cranny of Vaccine Corp. headquarters was on the back of his hand.

"Uncle, how do you know all of this?" she asked him.

"Being stuck in that cell for a year actually did have some benefits," he said between quick short breaths. "I could hear everything that everyone in a close enough proximity said. What were most helpful were the conversations between the guards. After a while, I could imagine an exact blueprint of the entire facility in my head."

Even with the map memorized, Vidya lost direction after traveling through dozens of hallways. Finally Samir stopped in front of a door that closely resembled the one that they had passed through before entering the restricted zone.

"She's in there." Samir looked at Vidya with an expression of fiery determination tinged with grief and fear.

"Here is where my vision comes in," Vidya said as she began examining the buttons on the lock keypad for finger oil residues. Within seconds Vidya had the four numbers that comprised the code and started to punch in combinations. In another half minute, the lock clicked open.

Without discussion, Samir opened the door and barged in. Vidya followed in so slowly, not knowing what to expect. What she saw was worse than she could ever imagine.

Jai finally saw a glint of light after traveling through a huge sea of darkness. It rejuvenated his energy and he sprinted toward the light source, hoping to find an exit. He found a wide-open set of double doors that lead outside, and so did the vacuum ducts. Jai positioned himself behind the wall next to the doors and peered through.

The ducts were shooting the canisters directly onto a thick cloth belt that led to the trunk of a large armored truck. He scoured the area with his eyes for any security guards that may have been lurking, but the only person around seemed to be the driver of the truck. From his vantage point, Jai could see that the driver was lightly armed with only a single pistol in his belt holster. *Dr. Faize must not want to draw too much attention to the truck so that the driver can slip secretly away.*

Jai darted over behind the truck, away from the driver's view. He then used his powerful legs to leap on top of the tall truck, landing lightly on his feet in order to not give away his presence. He crept silently over the metal trunk until he was directly over the driver's seat. Jai placed his hands on the side of the truck then dropped down next to the window.

The driver was caught by surprise. He did not even have time to draw his gun before Jai shot out his legs. Jai's feet smashed through the window glass, shards spraying everywhere before he planted a kick squarely on the driver's head. The driver was knocked out in less than a second.

Jai swung through the window into the trucks' interior. He examined an array of buttons, switches, and dials until he found the one he needed. Jai popped open the hood of the huge truck to expose its powerful engine. He then grabbed hold of the driver's unconscious body and half-dragged, half-carried it out of the truck far from harm's way.

Jai stayed back next to the driver and pulled out the handgun that Vidya had given to him. He gulped nervously. Jai had never touched a real gun before. *Just think of it as a paintball gun.* He tried to calm himself down. *I've been paintballing plenty of times.* Shakily, Jai pointed the gun at the bare engine of the armored truck and fired off a shot.

At first Jai thought he missed completely, but then a small wisp of smoke crept out of the engine. The smoke grew heavier and heavier, but still no fire was visible. Jai shot the engine once more, and then it erupted into flames. The fire quickly spread to the gas tank, and when it did, the entire truck exploded. Flames raced up the cloth belt into the duct system from which the virus canisters were being expelled. The enormous ball of fire expanded outwards, scorching everything in its path.

Fortunately, Jai estimated correctly and neither he nor the guard was seriously harmed. But the force was still enough to throw both of their bodies to the wall. Jai heard his cracked ribs jarring against each other, and winced at the searing pain. The fire diminished almost as quickly as it arrived, and all that was left of the truck was a charred frame.

As Jai hobbled back toward the lab, he began to smile through the pain. *At least I got the job done. That explosion was enough to kill the virus in those canisters at such intense heat. I just hope that Veer can take care of the rest.*

But meanwhile, Veer was already tired out and had not even destroyed two of the machines. He started to feel that his punches were getting weaker and less rapid. If he did not find another way soon, Dr. Faize's prediction would come true.

As he continued barraging the machine, a lone spark shot out. When Veer took a closer look, he discovered a small gap between the robotic arm and the lower half of the machine. Within the gap was a short stretch of unprotected wiring. Veer mustered his strength and aimed a punch straight at the gap. Several more sparks erupted from the contact point, and the machine immediately shut down. It was the shortcut he needed!

Veer's new discovery galvanized him and fueled his desire to destroy the machines. He sprinted from machine to machine, shooting out his fists at the weak points. Each punch was a one hit kill to the robotic arms. What was a long assembly line of virus manufacturers was quickly turning into a row of dilapidated useless metal. It did not even occur to Veer that his fists were bleeding, with gashes from sharp pieces of metal and lacerations from sharp wire, because he was so focused on his goal. He did not stop until he had taken down the very last machine.

Just as Veer rammed his fist into the last chunk of exposed wire, Jai limped through the crumbling hole in the wall from the dark bowels of the building. He grinned at the site of the demolished machinery then grasped his chest and grimaced.

"Jai, you okay?" Veer put his hand on his older brother's shoulder. "You don't look too good."

"Hey, at least I got the job done." Jai smiled through the pain of his cracked ribs. "You aren't such a pretty sight yourself."

Veer looked down at his bloodied fists and forearms, which were completely red by now. "No time to worry about it now. Nanna said we have got to do whatever it takes to destroy the remaining vats containing the virus."

"But how will we do that? Nanna told us that we had to get the cure and mix it into the vats in order to kill the remaining stores of the virus. But the cure is hidden somewhere and before Nanna could tell us how to find it, he left in a hurry to find Amma."

"The only person who would know where to find the cure is Dr. Faize himself. We could question . . ."

Before Veer could even finish his sentence, Jai dashed away toward the back of the lab. He ran to the spot that Dr. Faize had once lain unconscious after Veer had knocked him to the ground. But no one was in sight.

He got away! Jai's first instinct was to track him down, but he thought better of it. *We have got to take down this virus before we do anything else. But now how are we going to find the cure with Dr. Faize gone?* Jai's eyes quickly fell upon the answer. Sitting in the corner next to the stretcher laid Dr. Faize's laptop, which Jai suspected carried the vital information that he needed.

Jai began searching through the laptop's huge stores of files, calling upon all of the technological know-how that Samir had given him over the years. Veer finally arrived seconds later, panting and sweating.

"What are you doing?" he asked between gulping in gasps of fresh air.

"Looking for the cure. It has to be in here somewhere." But Jai was beginning to become disheartened as the computer combed through what seemed like an endless number of files. Finally the computer beeped. "Yes, got it!"

Jai opened up a blueprint of an aerial view of the very laboratory that they were sitting in. On the right-hand side of the screen was a bright orange circle, demarcating the cure. Jai immediately got up and sprinted over to the exact spot in the laboratory as shown on the computer. Veer groaned in exhaustion and followed him.

"Why isn't it here?" Jai was staring at a wall in front of him where the cure was supposed to be.

Veer took a closer look. A thin crack, barely visible to the human eye, stretched down the wall.

"Jai do you remember how Dr. Faize typed in something on his laptop, then all of those huge machines popped out of the ground?" His brother nodded. "Well, I think this is something similar. I think the cure is here, just concealed by a hidden door."

Jai returned with laptop in hand before Veer even finished. His hands flew over the keyboard, typing in commands to open up the door in every computer language he knew. But the door was not budging.

"How did he do it?" Jai continued trying every possible command. But he soon ran out of ideas and gave up. "Dr.

Faize must have had a special code that only he knew that could open the door. There is no way I can figure it out in time."

"The only other option is to use raw strength."

Veer threw his shoulder against the wall and pushed. He could feel his shoulder straining under the stress, but pain did not even matter to him anymore. He went to his very limit, thrusting his left arm against the door along with his right shoulder until they both burned with fiery pain. The door started to tremble under his power, first only cracking open an inch. Slowly that inch widened to a half foot, and the metal was bending precariously. Finally Veer heard a resounding snap as the door succumbed to his strength and crashed to the ground. Veer toppled over into the next room.

Jai followed him in to find a cramped room cooled to just slightly below room temperature. At the center of the room was a metal container with a glass cover at its front. Inside of it were rows of dozens of neatly aligned flasks, each filled to the brim with a neon orange liquid. *The cure!*

Veer opened the container and carefully handed the flasks over to Jai. When he had as many as he could possibly carry, Jai darted over to the vats at the opposite end of the lab. He went from vat to vat, pouring out a flask of the cure into each one. Every time the contents of the flasks were emptied, the clear liquid in vats bubbled violently then turned into a thick black glop. Jai shuttled from Veer and the vats until all of the viruses had been destroyed.

As Jai looked upon the containers filled with muck, he felt a feeling of satisfaction building in the pit of his stomach and warming his entire body. *We defeated the virus, and saved millions of human lives.* He was taken by surprise when Veer came up behind him and crushed him in a bear-like hug.

Jai grunted in pain. "Veer, my ribs," he said as the air was being forced out of his lungs.

"Sorry," Veer released his iron grip. "I didn't mean to. I just can't believe that we actually destroyed the virus."

"Me neither." Jai slapped his arm on his younger brother's shoulder. "But there is still one more thing we've got to do: save Amma."

Veer nodded. "You go on ahead and help Nanna and Vidya. I'll catch up."

After tearing through the meandering hallways at a breakneck speed, Jai arrived at the end of Samir's dirt trail. It stopped at an open door that led into an eerie room lit only by flickering red lights. He heard voices emanating from inside. It sounded as if a conflict was taking place.

Jai rushed inside and into a nightmare. Vidya and Samir stood at one side, watching in horror as Avery held Jyothi in a crushing grip with a gun placed behind her back. Jyothi's face was pale with fear while Avery, who usually showed no expression at all, had a wide grin plastered on his face. He was enjoying every moment of this.

"Why are you doing this?" Samir's voice was shaking. "I already told you that I can give you anything you want. You can have my money. You can take me back. Just don't hurt her." Samir took a step forward with his hands up, showing that he meant no harm.

Avery pressed down the safety switch on the pistol. "Come any closer and I'll kill her on the spot."

"Why are you doing this? Why do you want to hurt an innocent person?" Samir's voice started to show anger.

"Don't blame him. Blame me." Dr. Faize walked in grinning, exposing his bloody mouth that was missing teeth from when Veer had punched him. "I told him to do this."

"Why?" It was all that Samir could manage to utter.

Dr. Faize laughed, and then his face suddenly erupted with fury. "Because you ruined our plans. That virus could have made us the richest and most powerful company in the world. We could have had controlled national governments with the kind of money that this would have given us. You cost us trillions of dollars. That's why." Dr. Faize continued his rant. "And now you are going to pay for it with the life of your dear wife. What a shame, she really was a great employee." He mocked sadness. "Kill her." He then spat.

Jai reacted immediately and sprinted toward Avery. But not even Jai was faster than a bullet. Avery pulled the trigger with no remorse and a bullet shot through her chest. Jyothi's delicate frame fell like a ragdoll. She fell with a thump to the floor and her long black hair covered her face that held the expression of fear.

Veer arrived a second later to find his mother lying motionless on the floor. For a second, everything seemed to freeze. He saw the agony and grief in his father's face. Samir was not the determined man he was a moment before, but rather a broken shell of his former self. Jai was expressionless, obviously in shock. Then Veer looked over at Faize. His lips were curled, baring his blood-covered teeth and the corners of his mouth were twisted upward in a menacing grin. His eyes were wide open and showed vengeful elation. Veer felt the anger building inside of him.

Then everything erupted into action. Jai grabbed Avery's gun before he had the chance to shoot again. Veer took care of the rest. With a single uppercut he knocked Avery out cold. Now Faize was laughing maniacally. Veer could not stand the sound of his laugher. He swung his fist directly into Faize's temple. The evil leader of Vaccine Corp. slumped to the ground, unconscious.

Veer's anger was instantaneously replaced with sadness as he stared at his mother lying on the floor. Tears rolled down his cheek as he realized that he came so far to get one parent back just to lose another. He closed his eyes and wished that the gun never fired.

Then he heard a weak coughing noise. It gradually grew louder. Veer opened his eyes to see his mother gasping for breath. He couldn't believe it. She was alive!

"What happened?" Jyothi asked in a soft voice as she sat up.

Samir, Vidya, Veer, and Jai all smiled. It was the work of the good virus.

EPILOGUE

nu's old red station wagon sped down the highway leading home from the hospital. Jai sat alongside Anu in the front as Veer, Vidya, Jyothi, and Samir squeezed in the back. The bright sun shined upon them as a light breeze flowed in from the car's open windows. It was a perfect summer afternoon.

Anu constantly wiped away tears of grief-turned-into-happiness as she kept her eyes on the road. They had just finished filling her on the whole story starting with Samir's clues.

"Jai, Veer, Vidya, I am never letting Jyothi take you to work with her again." She laughed in between sniffles.

"Ma, it wasn't her fault," Vidya consoled her. "Aunty is still recovering."

"Actually I feel completely fine," Jyothi said as she held Samir's arm tightly. After being separated for over a year, Veer and Jai's parents could not be split. "I was shot fatally and somehow I survived and don't feel any pain whatsoever. But I still don't get why it happened."

"The mutated version of the Gaffa virus did it." Jai waved his hand through the cool summer breeze. "It found your biggest weakness, Amma, which was your weak immune system and slow recovery process. Then it turned that into an ability to heal even from the worst wounds."

Jyothi was so shocked that it took a moment for her to answer. "A virus did this to me? How come I didn't notice any symptoms before?" she wondered.

"I think with its high mutation rate, the time it takes for the virus to affect someone varies," Jai answered. "Veer, Vidya, and I first noticed our symptoms when we got that itchy rash months ago. And then the effects of the virus became more pronounced over time. I got faster and faster every day, Veer got stronger, and Vidya's eyesight got sharper. But the good virus took longer to affect you, Amma."

Veer nodded. "And we're lucky that it did because it saved your life. In fact, it probably helped us all stay alive during the fight at Vaccine Corp. in some way or another."

"I'm glad Dr. Faize didn't get his hands on the good virus," Samir said. "I regret telling him about the critical mutation that transformed the Gaffa virus into the good virus, but it was the only thing that I could think of to stall him. I heard you guys coming from your cell and knew that I had to buy some time. He didn't get the virus this time, but knowing what I heard from him while stuck in that cell, he'll be back for it soon." Then he turned toward Jyothi. "You have to quit your job at Vaccine Corp. Even though you had no idea about their scheme, I can't have you anywhere close to Dr. Faize."

"Don't worry, I'll quit." Jyothi seemed thankful to rid herself of the job.

The station wagon rolled down the long picturesque driveway leading home. Veer stared out at the beautiful trees lining their vast green backyard. He listened to the laughter of his friends and family and looked over at his smiling parents, finally together once again. After a long miserable year, Veer was happy.